Love & Life

Marlon McCaulsky
& Jarold Imes

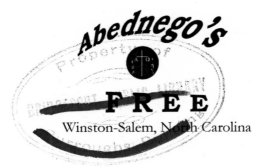

Abednego's

FREE

Winston-Salem, North Carolina

FREE

Abednego's Free, LLC
380-H Knollwood Street
Suite #138
Winston-Salem, North Carolina 27103

Book Credits
Editors: Kiera Davis, Tiffany Jones & Cedric Quincy
Cover Concept: Marlon McCaulsky, Jarold Imes & Teddy Petree
Cover Models: Terrance "TP" Petree & Ashley Hardesty
Cover Design & Photographer: Teddy Petree

10 9 8 7 6 5 4 3 2 1

ISBN 13: 978-934195-16-1
ISBN 10:   1-934195-16-2

Library of Congress Control Number: 2009924651

Printed in the United States of America

Real Love

By

Marlon McCaulsky

 *Chapter 1*

Welcome to Da Burg- Aug 20th 1994

Life is about change and for seventeen-year-old Raina Williams moving from Cleveland to St. Petersburg, Florida is the biggest change of her life. Raina stares outside the small window of the plane in her economy seat thinking about where her life is now. Now that she no longer has Rashad her ex-boyfriend in her life it didn't make sense to stay in Cleveland. Rashad was now at Ohio State Penitentiary for the next ten years after he got convicted being caught in his house with crack cocaine and a .45. That made moving a lot more easier. The soulful sounds of 'Real Love' by Mary J Bilge plays on her headphones and Raina asks herself what real love is for her. Her mother, sitting next to her started thinking about the adjustments she'll have to make in Florida. *This change might not be the best thing for Raina or me,* she thought.

Inside Tampa International Airport, Martin, Raina's father is waiting for them in the baggage claim area by the carousal. The carousal starts to move and suitcases and baggage start to appear from behind the black flaps on the walls. The electronic sign above the carousal says American Airlines Flight 874 from Cleveland. People from the flight start to come down the escalators and Martin sees Tonya and Raina coming.

"Hey don't I know you two from somewhere?"

"You do look like some guy I used to mess with," Tonya says to him.

"This never gets old to you two does it," Raina says to

them embarrassed.

"I miss you too baby girl," Martin says and hugs them both.

"How was the flight?"

"It was aight." Raina says to him.

"Good. You're gonna like it down here, trust me."

Tonya forces a smile on her face.

"Did our luggage come out yet?" Tonya asks him.

"No not yet."

"How are we gonna get all our stuff into your car dad?"

"Don't worry about that my friend Shawn from down the street drove his Rodeo here."

The baggage carousal rotates and more suitcases start to appear from behind the black rubber curtain. After a brief wait Raina spots their luggage and Martin grabs their cases off of the carousal.

As they drive over the Howard Franklin Bridge, Raina stares out into the bay wondering what her life is going to be like down here. It's totally different from Cleveland and she doesn't even have Joy or LeTasha by her side to hang with. But being in Cleveland was nothing but drama so being away from everything and everybody is just what she needed. Shawn drives them over I - 275 South and exits off at Exit 6 and drives into the upscale neighborhood of Pinellas Point. They pull into the driveway of a two-story brick house.

"Come on let's get you guys settled in," Martin opens the front door and Tonya and Raina are blown away by the size of the living room.

"Whoa. This is nice," Raina utters.

Her dad smiles, "Just wait till you see your room."

Raina heads up the spiral stairs to her new bedroom.

"So how do you like it baby?" Martin asks Tonya.

"It's nice Martin. It looks bigger then the pictures you sent me."

"I'm glad you came baby," Martin says to her.

"I love you Martin. We're going to make this work."
Tonya says to him and he kisses her.

Raina walks into her new bedroom and sees that her dad has already decorated her room with pictures of her friends and one of her and Rashad together on the dresser. Raina picks up the picture frame of Rashad and her, stares at it for a second, and then puts it in the drawer.

After unpacking, Raina lies on her bed listening to her Sony CD player headphones trying not to think about Rashad. She hears a knock on the door.

"Come in," Raina says.

Her dad comes in and closes the door.

"So how do you like it?"

She looks around the room, "I like it a lot."

"I know this is a big change for you. This being your senior year and leaving your friends behind is a big adjustment."

"Dad, don't worry about me. After the drama I had up in Cleveland I'm ready for a change. Besides I know this is a big promotion for you," Raina says to him.

"I'm glad you understand how important this move was for us. I missed you baby girl."

"I missed you too daddy," Raina says and gives him a hug.

"Hey, Shawn and his daughter Sheena are downstairs. You two are going to be going to the same school. Do you wanna come say hello?"

"Sure why not."

They walk downstairs and Raina sees Sheena sitting on the white leather couch with her dad, Shawn.

"Raina, this is Sheena," Martin introduces her.

"Hey what's up," Sheena says to her.

"Hey," Raina replies shyly.

Raina knows that sometimes she comes off standoffish when she meets new people but it's just that she's trying to get to know them so she hopes that Sheena isn't offended. Sheena was wearing a black Gap shirt that hugged her well-endowed breasts, a pair of dark blue jeans and all white Nikes on her feet. Sheena was a beautiful coffee brown girl with black hair that hung in candy curls just past her shoulders.

"Well I guess I should be the first person to officially welcome you to Da Burg," Sheena jokes to her. Sheena looked friendly and gave Raina no bad vibes.

"Da Burg huh? This is like a new world to me."

"Well being that you're new to around here let me be your guide. Every girl should know where the mall is," Sheena says to her and she laughs. "Is that ok dad?"

"Oh yeah go ahead. Do you need some money?"

She shakes her head, "Nah, I'm good."

"See ya daddy," Sheena says to her dad.

"Please don't hurt me to bad with the credit card Sheen," Shawn begs her.

"Daddy you know how I do it. See ya," Sheena quips and walks out with Raina.

A few minutes later Sheena is driving down 22nd Ave in her dad's Rodeo and looks over at Raina staring out the window.

"You miss Cleveland?" Sheena asks.

"Is it that obvious?"

"A little. Don't mind me I'm like a little chatterbox. I never know when to shut up," Sheena jokes to her.

"I don't mind ... you remind me of my friend Tasha."

"That's good. Well let me warn you, St. Pete ain't known for being the jump off city."

"Don't worry, about it. I'm looking forward to a change of pace. So who are we meeting up here?"

"My boyfriend Marcus and his friends Dan and Cory."

"Any of them cute?" Raina inquires.

"Oh yeah, just be careful around the real horny one," Sheena warns her.

Raina frowns, "Horny one? Which one is that?"

"Oh, you'll know him as soon as you see him."

♥♥♥

In the middle of Tyrone Square Mall's food court Dan and Marcus are eating some orange chicken while Cory sips on a soda. Cory's stomach growls as he watches Dan and Marcus devour their food.

"Yo Dan, you gonna eat that?" Cory asks.

"Naw dog, I just like the way it looks on my plate," Dan replies sarcastically.

"Come on man just give me that piece right there."

"If you touch my food, I'm gonna hurt you," Dan warns him.

"Don't even look over here man, you should have saved your money instead of buying them ugly ass Jordan's," Marcus states to him.

Cory stares at him, "They ain't ugly, they cost $150.00!"

"Ain't nobody told you to spend your whole check on that shit," Dan says to him.

"I don't know why you be trying to act like a baller all the time," Marcus says to Cory.

"Man I got an image I got to maintain for the ladies. That's how I be pulling them hoes. You don't know about that though," Cory cockily retorts.

"Wow ... that's the reason why we keep you around. Where else are we gonna get these thought provoking quotes that you just spit out that retarded little brain of yours," Dan quips.

"What ... man I'm trying to show you how to get that quality ass."

"Show who? We got girlfriends," Marcus snaps.

Cory glares at Marcus, "Yeah but have you tapped Sheena's fine ass yet? No."

Dan takes another bite of his food, "So you got the new Jordan's but you can't buy any food? So now you're ballin' on a budget," Dan asks him.

"Man this is just a temporary situation you have to make sacrifices in order to be a playa. It's a lifestyle … an art form Y'all just don't understand. Y'all on lock down, while I got all these girls to holla at," Cory proclaims.

"Shut up you broke bastard," Marcus yells at him.

Lissa Norman, Dan's girlfriend walks up to the table wearing a cute little color block summer dress that hugs her slender curvy frame. Her long black hair flows behind her as if it were caught by the wind. Lissa was fine that much is undeniable. With shopping bags in hand, over size sunglasses on, spending her parent's money was second nature. And she's been Dan's lady for the past year.

"Daniel, I'm gonna check that new store out."

"You gonna be long?" Dan asks already knowing she will.

"No, I would ask you to go with me but I know you don't like shopping."

"No…He hate's shopping with you," Marcus mumbles to himself.

"What was that Marcus?" Lissa quickly fires back.

"Oh, nothing Lissa you go enjoy yourself," Marcus says patronizingly.

"That's what I thought. I'll see ya in a minute baby," Lissa kisses Dan and she walks toward the department store.

"Man why you always messing with her like that?" Dan asks Marcus.

"You're my dawg but Lissa is more stuck up then a tampon dawg."

Dan can't help but laugh.

"And that's why I don't have a girlfriend," Cory proudly says to them.

"You don't have a girlfriend cuz' nobody wants your stink ass!"

Just as the guys begin to crack on each other, Sheena and

Raina walk through the mall doors. Dan sees Raina immediately. She sees him and they lock eyes. Her dark blue jeans were like a second skin wrapped around her thick thighs. Her tight round ass moves in a rhythmic motion with every step. Her full cleavage bounced in her scarlet red V-neck t-shirt, her face was flawless. Dan, however wasn't the only one blown away by Raina's beauty.

"Oh snap, look at the dime piece with Sheena, who is that?" Cory asks.

"You got me, never seen her before," Marcus says to him.

"She got a pretty face and a bangin' body. I'm gonna have her on my team, take notes."

"Shut up," Marcus and Dan say together.

"What's up fellas, hey baby," Sheena says to Marcus.

Marcus gets up and kisses her.

"Aye, this is Raina, she just moved in down the street from me."

Raina smiles and waves her hand, "Hey."

"What's up girl," Cory jumps up and shakes her hand.

"Hey how are you doing?" Dan says to her.

Raina takes in Dan's handsome face and defined chest and her already protruding nipples became hard. His hair was cut in a fade with endless waves. His neatly lined sideburns connected to his beard on his cocoa brown skin. This boy was fine. His lips were full and succulent; and she could imagine how they would feel on her lips.

"Good," Raina says with a smile. She can't believe that she just let herself get so aroused by a guy she just met.

"Raina, this is Marcus, Cory and Dan," Sheena introduces her to the guys.

Cory like a lion pouncing on a gazelle in the wild steps to Raina, "So where are you from?"

"Cleveland."

"That's nice, have a seat," Cory says to her and pulls out a chair.

Raina looks at Sheena to let her know she figured out

who *Mr. Horny* was. He wasn't ugly, just not her type, too skinny for her liking.

"Are you gonna go to Lakewood high too?" Dan inquires.

"Yeah."

"We all go there," Sheena says to her.

"Yeah, so we'll show you around," Dan stares at her beautiful round butterscotch face. Her wavy black hair was pulled back into a ponytail. His manhood uncontrollably hardens in his pants as lustful thoughts pop into his mind.

"Thanks."

Cory glares at Dan as if he's cock blocking him.

"Yeah I'll show you all the hot spots," Cory interjects with a corny line.

"Anyway, what y'all about to get into?" Sheena asks Marcus.

"I think we might see a movie."

Lissa returns to the table and sees the way Dan is looking at this new girl. And like most wild animals Lissa is very protective of her territory.

"They don't have anything good in there. I'm ready to go," Lissa says to Dan totally ignoring everybody else at the table.

"We just got here."

"Baby there ain't nothing here," Lissa replies to Dan then looks over her shoulder at Raina. "Oh hello, who are you?"

"That's Raina, she just moved down here from Cleveland," Sheena informs her.

"Oh, nice shirt, where did you get that?" Lissa probes examining her from head to toe.

"In Cleveland, a shop called-"

"Hmm….Interesting, Daniel are you ready to go?" Lissa dismissively says cutting Raina off and then looks back at Dan. Not wanting to argue in front of everybody he concedes to her wishes.

"Yeah well, I'll see y'all later."

"Aight dog," Marcus says to him.

"Peace," Cory shouts then grins at Raina.

"See ya, Dan," Sheena says and shakes her head.

"It was nice to meet you," Dan says with a smile to Raina.

"Yeah, you too."

Lissa starts to walk to the exit, "Daniel, come on."

Dan gets up from the table to catch up with her.

"I can't believe my boy is letting her run him like that," Marcus retorts.

"Don't mind that bitch. I don't know what he sees in her," Sheena says to Raina.

"Biiitcch," Marcus yells.

"It's alright, I know her type," Raina informs them.

"Anyway, let's get back to you," Cory says and takes her hand.

♥♥♥

After dropping Lissa home, Dan went to his home in Lakewood Estates a middle class suburb in St. Petersburg. Dan walks in the front door and sees his mom Monica cooking dinner. He strolls into the spacious kitchen and sits at the island.

"Hey mom."

"Hey baby."

"Dang mom that smells good is that what I think it is?"

"Yes it is, pot roast."

"I swear I ain't never leaving home if you keep on cooking like this."

"You're just like you're father when it comes to food."

John, Dan's dad walks into the kitchen with a magazine in his hand.

"It runs in the family," He says and kisses Monica. He walks over to the island. "Just like talent."

"They printed my article?"

"Look for yourself," John says proudly. Dan reads his

short story in the magazine.

"Oh man this is so tight they printed it!"

"Congratulation's baby."

"Thanks mom, I submitted this story months ago. I didn't think they were going to publish it."

"I told you to have faith in yourself," John says to him. Dan smiles and sits back down and reads his article.

Sheena drops Raina off in front of her house.

"Thanks for taking me out." Raina says to her.

"No problem, so I'll pick ya up tomorrow morning for school alright?"

"Yeah that's cool."

"I'll call ya before I come over."

"Okay, see ya later." Raina replies as she gets out of the car. Raina walks into the house and goes upstairs and sees her mom sitting on the bed by herself.

"Hey mom, where's dad?"

"He went out."

Raina can hear the tension in her voice and can tell that she's upset.

"Are you alright mom?"

"Yeah, I'm fine, how do you feel?"

"Alright, I had fun with Sheena and her friends. Well most of them."

"That's good, but how do you feel about being here," Tonya asks Raina wearily and smiles.

"This is a chance of a lifetime for dad, and after all the things that happened back home, I'm ready for a change."

She takes her hand, "Okay, but if you need to talk I'm right here."

"I know mom. It's going to be fine," Raina gives her a hug.

Chapter 2

By the lockers in the hallway, Dan, Marcus, and Cory post up watching everybody come in on the first day of school. This is the same spot they always stand at to check out all the hot, new girls on campus. Lakewood has had the nickname 'Hollywood High' since the '80's because of how fly everybody dressed. You had to come fly or get clowned. Most of the guys wore Tommy Hilfiger, Nikes, and FUBU while a good number of girls wore dresses just high enough to show a little thigh or low cut shirts with enough cleavage to get away with it.

"Damn, there's so much stray ass all over the place this year. This don't make no sense," Cory says.

"Yeah, just like you," Marcus responded.

"Stop hating on a brotha. Ooohhh, looks like Tangela grew out of that training bra this year ... and filled out just right."

"Sheena is giving that new girl a ride today right?" Dan asks Marcus.

"Yeah, that's what she said."

Cory looks at them and grins, "Oh yeah, Cleveland, I gotta holla at her quick before these other niggas see her."

"Her name's Raina ya know," Dan informs him.

"Whatever," Cory replies.

Sheena and Raina walk through the hall. All the guys stop to look at them. Raina is wearing her hair down today parted in the middle. She looks like she could have been Aaliyah's twin sister. They walk over to the guys and Dan and Raina lock eyes once again. The chemistry is undeniable. Once again Dan is blown away by how good she looks in them jeans. Raina's hips rocked from side to side with every step. Her body was just amazing to watch move.

"What's up guys?" Sheena asks them.

"Hey y'all," Raina says to every body.

"Hey, how you doing Raina?" Dan asks her.

"Pretty good."

"Hey boo, what's up Raina?" Marcus says as he hugs Sheena.

"Oh, there she is. What's up Rainy?" Cory quips trying to be cute.

"Don't call me that, they use to say that shit to me all the time in middle school I couldn't stand it," Raina snaps annoyed.

"Sorry man, you know I'm just playing," Cory quickly apologizes.

"Did you get your schedule yet?" Dan asks Raina.

"Yeah I got biology first period."

He smiles, "Welcome to 'Hollywood High.'"

"Thanks," Raina says to him and can't help but smile at him.

Lissa walks up to Dan and ignores everybody else.

"Hey baby, you ready to go to class?" She then turns and looks at the others, "Oh, hey y'all," Lissa dryly says to them as if she's doing them all a favor in even acknowledging their presence.

As if they all rehearsed it, they all say her name in unison dryly, "Hey Lissa."

Lissa turns her head and looks them up and down knowing that none of them likes her.

"Well, good to see you too, Daniel can we go?"

"Yeah, in a minute."

Dan knows he's been looking like a punk in front of the fellas and wants it to stop now. Lissa sensed that Dan is growing more and more annoyed with her demands. But she also knew she can catch more flies with honey then vinegar, more accurately, her honey.

"Hey, my mom is working late tonight," Lissa, says to Dan, dropping a hint to what she wants to do. Even though Dan may be annoyed with Lissa's rude behavior at times he realized she was still a dime. Lissa runs her fingers down his chest and gives Dan a closer look at her her luscious cleavage in her summer dress.

"Really how late?" Dan inquisitively asks.

"Late enough." Lissa says and licks her lips.

Raina has a look of disappointment hearing them talk to each other like that and looks at her school schedule, "Hey does anybody know where room 102 is?"

"I'll walk you down there," Cory offers.

"Don't worry about it Cory I'm going that way," Sheena interjects wanting to keep Cory away from her.

"Oh yeah, you're the new girl," Lissa recalls as if she forgot. Raina nods as if she knows Lissa is going to say some smart-ass remark to her.

"Another interesting outfit ... where do you find them at?" Lissa sarcastically retorts.

"Hey, chill out," Dan says to Lissa, trying to defuse the moment. To everybody's surprise Raina doesn't back down.

"I just got an original style, not everybody has originality."

Lissa looks stunned by her response. Marcus and Cory turn and laugh to each other.

"Oh hell naw," Cory says laughing.

"Nice facial," Marcus utters under his breath. Dan lightly elbows Marcus and puts his arm around Lissa quickly and starts to walk away.

"Let's go baby, alright y'all later."

"Fine by me." Lissa spits and glares at Raina.

"We better get going too. So we'll see ya at lunch?" Sheena asks Marcus.

"Yeah meet us outside." Marcus says and kisses her. Sheena and Raina walk down the hallway to her bio class.

"So what's up with you two?" Sheena asks Raina.

"Nothing, I just don't like being called Rainy."

"I wasn't talking about Cory, I meant Dan."

"Oh, he's alright, but he's with Lissa remember?"

"She ain't right for him, besides I see the way you two were looking at each other."

"What?! You're seeing things," Raina adamantly denies.

"Yeah, I know what I saw. I think you two would be good together."

"Tell that to Lissa. What's her problem anyway?"

Sheena rolls her eyes, "That bitch! Please! She got too many to list. Dan is just a little confused by his hormones right now."

"He's cute but I ain't trying to get involve with anybody right now."

"Did you have a bad relationship before?"

Raina nods her head, "Yeah something like that."

"What happened?"

"He was the thuggish type and he got caught with some weight on him."

"How much?"

"Enough to get him seven years."

Sheena grimaces, "Ewww, I'm sorry about that but you just gotta get back on it."

"Girl it's been about nine and a half months since I been back on it," Raina says laughing.

"Damn! Isn't it like an earring hole it'll…"

"I got cobwebs down there," she jokes and Sheena laughs. "What about you and Marcus? You two … ah …"

"No … we haven't. Well … I never have," Sheena says timidly.

"Does he want to?" Raina asks.

"Yeah, but he hasn't come out and said it but he's a guy, I know he wants to." Sheena confirms.

"How long have you two been together?"

"About two months."

"Do you want to do it?" Raina asks her.

"Yeah … but I'm kinda scared to ya'know? Did you and

your ex do it?"

"Yeah, he was my first. It was what I wanted to do. I loved him. But trust me Sheena don't do it until you're ready to."

"Oh trust me … I've taken so many cold showers that my dad thinks I'm the most hygiene conscious girl in the world," Sheena says laughing.

After school, Dan is taking a sexual education class in Lissa's bedroom studying her anatomy. Unlike most girls in high school, Lissa was not shy about having sex. When it came to getting her freak on she had no problem throwing down. Riding cowgirl is her favorite position. She loved the deep penetration and the intense sensation her clitoris would feel, rubbing and grinding up and down Dan's thick brown shaft. Even more then the stimulation she got from it, Lissa loved being in control. Making Dan moan out loud turned her on even more. Lissa turned around and began to ride Dan backwards, cowgirl style, he watched himself slide in and out of her moistness between her soft curvy butt cheeks. She rolled her hips slowly and tightens her walls. Dan utters out softly. Lissa then bounced up and down faster flexing her walls around him making Dan explode profusely into his condom. Dan moans as Lissa leans forward and kisses his lips.

"You feel so good inside of me baby," Lissa says to him and Dan closes his eyes and enjoys his orgasm. Afterward, Dan is lying in bed with Lissa looking at the ceiling lost in thought. Lissa is lying on top of his chest tracing her fingers around his chest.

"Damn, that shit felt so good. I can't wait to be away in college. Being in a dorm room instead of creeping around like this," Lissa says to him.

"Yeah right."

"What are you thinking about?"

"I didn't tell you yet, but my article got printed."

"Really, that's nice," Lissa says nonchalantly.

"Nice... that's it, *nice?*" Dan says irritated.

"What do you want me to do?"

Dan shrugs, "Nothing I guess, I was just expecting you to be a little more excited for me."

"I am. I know you're going to do bigger things with your life."

Dan is disappointed by her reaction.

"I was just thinking about what I thought I would be doing after I got out of school. When you where a little girl what did you wanna be?"

"I don't know, maybe Barbie or something like that. I just like the way she had everything she wanted. Why?"

Dan shakes his head, "Barbie? I guess that makes me Ken."

"I was seven years old silly, but I do know what we want," Dan is quiet, looks at her, and then starts to get out of bed.

"I was just wondering. Anyway, I better go before your mom comes home."

"Call me when you get home okay?"

"Yeah alright."

Dan comes home and goes through the den and sees his dad, John, watching TV and sits down next to him. They've always been close.

"Hey dad."

"What's going on son?"

"Nothing much."

"Oh, your girl Lissa just called for you a few minutes ago."

Dan sighs, "Already, I just saw her."

"Sounds like you got the poor girl sprung."

"Yeah I guess," Dan says laughing.

"That's how we Kelly's put it down." John says proudly and gives Dan some dap.

"Dad, can I ask you a question, seriously?" John turns down the TV.

"Yeah, what is it?"

"How did you know mom was the one for you?" Dan asks him.

"I think I had to ask myself has anybody ever made me feel the way she makes me feel. When I had that answer there was no doubt in my mind. Do you think Lissa's the one?" John asks him.

"I don't know, how do you know when it's real?" Dan asks him.

"When it's real son, you won't even have to ask," John says to him.

"Thanks dad."

Dan walks in his room and sits at his desk. He takes out a writing pad and opens it we see the title "Missing Heart" and he turns to the spot where he left off and writes:

> "What's Real? Love, lust, desire, passion how do I know the differences between them? If I see it can I reach it? If I touch it would I feel it? Or is it all just an illusion I created in my head?"

He stops writing and stares at the paper.

Chapter 3

<u>*Drinking UNO- November 10th 1994*</u>

A few months into the school year and Raina decided to keep her distance from Dan. *No need to be around someone you can't have,* she thought. Dan and Lissa are walking together down the hallway between fourth and fifth period.

"Hey, I think were going to go by Sheena's house tonight and hang out. Do you wanna come with me?"

Lissa rolls her eyes, "What are they going to be doing?"

"I think they're going to play Uno or something. Just hanging out."

"Uno, oh well, I'll pass. They don't like me anyway."

"You never gave them a chance to like you. If you didn't come at them with so much attitude-"

"They're your friends not mines, go if you want just call me when you get in," Lissa says dismissively.

"Alright," Dan says nonchalantly.

"Talk to you later baby," She kisses him.

"Yeah see ya."

Dan goes into the library, takes out a book from his bag, and walks to a table. He sees Raina sitting by herself reading a book and goes to join her. Raina looks up from her book and smiles.

"Hey! What's up?"

Raina grins, "Nothing much."

"Is this seat taken?"

"No. Do you usually come in here?"

"Yeah, it's quiet, so I like to read in here?"

"*House of Sand and Fog,* you're actually reading that?"

Raina asks him surprised.

"Yeah."

Raina squints, "Is that required reading for English III?"

"No, I like Andre Dubus work. Don't look so shocked, I do read."

"No, I didn't mean it like that, it's just not too many guys our age read books like that."

"There's a lot you don't know about me," He says with a smile.

Raina blushes and shakes her head, "I'm sure."

"For example, I bet you didn't know that I've read your book there."

"*Disappearing Acts*, You've read this?"

"One of my favorite Terry McMillan books, I like it better than *Waiting to Exhale*."

Raina is shocked by his book knowledge.

"Wow, I'm impressed. How come you're such a book worm?"

"Oh, it's a fetish." Dan says.

"Fetish, what other fetishes do you have?" Raina inquires further.

"Nothing I can show you here in public," Dan says with a smile.

"That's too much information," Raina says and she looks in her book.

Dan decides to push her buttons further with some questions of his own.

"So are you turning into a Terry McMillan character?"

"What ... no! Why would you even say that?"

"It's just most girls that read her books identify with a character of hers."

"Well no, I'm not a Terry McMillan character I'm just still looking for the right man. I mean... I'm not looking for a man now."

Dan can see that she's fluster and continues.

"So who is the right kind of guy for Raina Williams?"

Raina looks into Dan's eyes deeply.

"Someone who's going to be himself all the time ... who's not going to put up a front around other people ya'know?"

"Yeah, I think I do."

"I guess I'm still trying to get what you got with Lissa," Raina says flipping the awkwardness back on him. Dan doesn't respond right away.

"Yeah I guess, so are you going to be at Sheena's tonight?"

"Yeah, I'll be there."

"Good."

♥♥♥

That night Raina goes over to Sheena's house. As usual Sheena's dad is in Tampa for the weekend with his new girlfriend, which leaves Sheena alone to entertain some guest. Of course he checks up on her with phone calls but Sheena has never given her dad reason to worry and he trusts his daughter. But even the most responsible teenage daughters do a little dirt now and then. Sheena and Raina are in the den watching BET.

"He called me a Terry McMillan character."

Sheena doesn't say anything and looks the other way. Raina looks at her waiting for a response.

"You think I'm like that too," Raina asks stuned.

"Well you do kinda fit the description."

Raina's jaw drops, "I don't believe this!"

"It's not that bad you just need to meet the right guy maybe you already have. Besides you can't see he's flirting with you?" Sheena says to her.

"There you go again Dan has a lady."

TLC's 'Creep' video starts to play on TV.

"I'm just tryin' to point out the obvious to you. Oh they're playing the new TLC video. I love that dance they do."

"Yeah I know the steps," Raina says to her.

Raina gets up and shows Sheena the dance moves and Sheena gets up and does it too. They hear the doorbell and Sheena answers the door. She let's Marcus, Dan and Cory inside.

"Come in guys."

Marcus gives her a kiss and stares at her ass as they follow her inside.

"Where's my girl at?" Cory asks.

"Your girl?" She replies sarcastically.

"Yeah you know, Cleveland," Cory adds.

"Got to keep on reminding him she has a name," Dan informs Sheena.

"Hey y'all," Raina says.

"What's up?" Dan says to her.

"Damn, girl you looking kinda good tonight," Cory affirms with a grin on his face.

"Thank you Cory," Raina says to him.

Dan sees the TLC 'Creep' video playing.

"This is like the new ladies anthem. *'So I creep... yeah just keep it on the down low'* that's some scary shit."

"Hey sometimes you gotta do what you gotta do," Raina says to him.

Sheena smiles at them both. They all sit around the coffee table on the couch, "Alright, let's get the game started."

"Everybody knows how to play UNO but this time there's a twist, every time you get a 'Skip' or 'Draw' card you have to take a shot of this ..."

Sheena pulls out from under the coffee table.

"Bacardi," Raina says with dread.

"Oh, man I love where this is going," Marcus says.

"Hell yeah," Cory yells!

"Oh, shit. Where did you get that Sheen?"

"Dan you know my dad has like a liquor store in his cabinet. I pulled this from the back. He won't even miss it."

"Now every time you pull a 'Draw 2' or '4' you gotta take the same amount of shots."

"You gotta be out of your mind girl, we gonna get messed up before the end of the first game!"

"That's the main idea Dan. I'll deal," Sheena says happily.

They start to play and everybody taking shots. Dan is sitting next to Raina and keeps on throwing out 'Draw 4' and 'Draw 2's.' Raina and Sheena are taking the most shots and are quickly getting drunk. Cory is faking his shots by spiting most of it back in his cup. Dan and Marcus are winning most of the games.

Marcus takes another card from the deck and smiles, "Yo D, I'm about ready to set it off you ready?"

Dan smirks and looks at Raina, "Yeah, let's do this."

"Do what?" Raina nervously asks.

"Bring the pain!" Cory yells.

"Marcus, I swear if you put down what I think you're gonna put down …" Sheena warns him.

"Sorry baby, all's fair in love and UNO."

Marcus throws down a red 'Draw 2' to Sheena.

"Oh hell naw!"

Sheena throws out a red 'Draw 2' to Cory.

"Boom," Cory yells.

Cory puts down a blue 'Draw 2' to Dan. He starts to sing Phil Collins 'In the Air Tonight.'

"Oh God no. I can't drink no more," Raina says miserably. "Just put the damn card down," Raina demands.

Dan puts down another blue 'Draw 2' to Raina. She shakes her head in disbelief.

"That is so messed up," Sheena yells.

"I told you I was going to set it off," Marcus says laughing.

"Check your cards again, you don't got a 'Wild' card or 'Draw 2' in there?" Sheena asks Raina.

"Nope."

"So that's eight shots huh," Dan retorts sarcastically.

"Shut up Dan," Sheena yells.

"It's all good," Raina says to him.

Dan starts the chant, "Chug, chug, chug!" Marcus joins in, "Chug, chug, chug!" Cory also chants along, "Chug, chug, chug!"

Raina takes her glass and pours out the shots. She drinks them one by one with each shot burning as they go down.

"You all right Ray?" Sheena asks.

Raina shakes her head and grimaces, "I'm cool."

"You sure?" Dan inquires.

"Yeah." Raina picks up her cards.

"So Ray, do you have a boyfriend up north?" Cory asks.

"Not really."

"Not really, what happened?"

"Cory, where's your nose at?" Sheena asks him. Sheena takes another drink of her Bacardi.

"It's all right he's in prison," Raina replies.

"Damn, that's messed up. I'm sorry to hear that," Dan says.

"What he do?" Marcus asks.

"He got caught selling."

"Do y'all still talk?"

"No not really."

"Y'all all in her business," Sheena yells at them.

"It's cool, ever since he went in I haven't been talking to anybody. I'm not trying to get deep with nobody I guess."

"You can't push everybody away. You gotta start seeing other people and move on," Cory says hoping she'll move on to him.

"I know, I guess it's easier that way."

"What made y'all come down here?" Dan asks Raina.

"My dad got a surgical position at Bay Front. It was a few months after Rashad went in. Plus his baby mama was trying to start shit with me."

"For what?" Sheena slurs.

"She was saying if he was with her he would've never got busted."

"That's so stupid," Sheena yells.

"I don't have time for the drama."

With the Bacardi freely coursing through her system Sheena gets on her knees.

"What are you doing?" Marcus asks.

"We need to pray," Sheena announces.

"Pray?" Dan asks confused.

"Yeah man, Raina needs a higher power to bless her," Sheena seriously says. Sheena looks up in the air and everybody looks up in a weird way.

"You are tore up," Marcus utters.

"SHHHH! We are praying! Everybody close your eyes," Sheena demands.

"What the hell?" Cory looks at her oddly. "Y'all crazy."

"Heavenly Father, we ask you to move in sista Raina's life …" Sheena says in her Pentecostal church voice.

"Marc, get ya girl," Dan says.

"Me? And do what?"

"SHHHH! We ask that you remove all bustas, dogs, and fake hoes from her life…"

"Can I get a witness?" Raina chimes in.

"Lawd! Move your healing hands over her!"

"Say it again," Raina adds rocking back and forth.

"Move over her," Sheena shouts really feeling the Spirit and the Bacardi.

"Y'all are so going to hell," Dan says shaking his head.

"Show us your power in Jesus name!"

"Amen, sista Sheena," Raina yells.

"Amen," Sheena says emotionally.

"Can we please play the game now?" Marcus asks.

"Yeah let's do this man," Cory adds.

"What are you talking about Cory? Your non-drinking ass ain't drank shit all night," Dan shouts.

Cory frowns, "Whatever!"

They continue to play and Dan pulls a card.

He looks at Raina and smiles, "I hate to do it to you but …"

Dan throws down a 'Draw 4' to Raina.

"Oh no, I can't drink anymore!"

"Come on girl! I can't get drunk by myself! But we gotta do this! I'll do it with you," Sheena says completely drunk.

"Hell no, I can't," Raina exclaims.

"I knew you were soft." Dan says mockingly. Raina looks at him, picks up the glass and Bacardi, and takes four shots back to back.

"That's it I'm out, I gotta drive home," Cory says.

"Alright, it's over. Hey Dan can you make sure Raina gets home safe," Sheena purposely says to him.

"I don't need help I'm fine," Raina slurs out. She gets up, tries to walk, and stumbles over into Dan's arms.

"Fine. Yeah I'll make sure she gets home," Dan says to Sheena.

"Alright, maybe I'm a little drunk. But I was there with you girl," Raina says to Sheena.

"Like a solider!"

"Aight Captain Inebriated let's go to the car," Dan says to her.

"Bye y'all!"

Sheena sits back down on the couch and touches her mouth.

"Oh my God?" She says worried.

"What's wrong baby?" Marcus asks her concern.

"I can't feel my teeth." Sheena says scared. Marcus shakes his head and walks away.

Outside Sheena's house, Dan is helping Raina walk to his Ford Probe. She has her arms around his shoulder taking baby steps.

"That's it one, foot then the other one."

"Oh, man, I think I got it," Raina says to him. Dan gets her inside the car and starts to drive her home. He rolls down the window for her.

"Damn girl, I didn't think you were gonna do those last shots."

"I had to show you I wasn't soft!" Raina yells sarcastically to him.

"Alright, I'm sorry, I underestimated you. But you don't

have to prove anything to me."

"I know, right here."

Dan pulls in front of her house.

"Are you sure, you can make it in?"

Raina tries to pull herself together then looks at him, "Nope."

Dan gets out of the car and helps her to her front door. "Goodnight." She slips and Dan catches her, their lips are inches away from each other.

"I got you," Dan whispers to her softly. Face to face, staring into his big brown eyes, Raina gives into her temptation and gives him a soft lippy kiss then pulls away slowly. She shock by what she just done and Dan is also speechless by what just happen.

"Bye," Raina says to him.

"Bye."

Raina opens the door and goes inside. Dan walks away slowly; and confused but happy. Raina leans against the door stunned at what just happened. She then walks pass her parents room and goes into her room. Martin sees her stagger by and knocks on her door softly.

"Raina, are you all right?"

She's in bed under the covers. "I'm fine Dad."

"Had a little too much to drink huh?"

"You're not going to tell mom are you?"

"No, I remember my teen drinking years very painfully. Besides the monster hangover you're going to have in the morning will teach you a lesson. Just don't make a habit out of this."

"Don't have to worry about that. I haven't seen you much the past couple of days, working over time?" Raina asks him.

"Yeah, had a lot of work to catch up on lately, go to sleep baby girl."

"Night."

He kisses her head and walks out. Raina lies in bed and thinks about what happen with Dan and smiles.

Chapter 4

<u>*Love Hangover- November 11th 1994*</u>

In the kitchen, Dan's mom is making breakfast and his dad is reading a *Jet* magazine as usual. Dan walks in and sits at the table.

"Morning Dad."

"Morning Dan."

"Morning baby, do you want some breakfast?" Monica asks Dan.

"Yeah, can I get some bacon too?"

"Okay, is there something on your mind?"

"Yeah you look more confused than usual."

"Thanks, but I'm alright."

"Boy, I know you better then you think, talk." Monica says to him.

Dan leans back in his chair and smiles.

"This girl that moved in down the street, we're friends but I'm trying to figure out some of the things she does."

"Oh, so you're trying to figure her out."

"Good luck," John says sarcastically.

"Quiet John, women are not that hard to figure out, you just have to be observant and sensitive," Monica says.

"Is that how Dad got you?"

"That and I put that thing on-"

Monica cuts her eyes at him, "You finish that sentence and you won't be putting that thing on anything for awhile."

John swallows hard then looks at Dan, "I meant I did the same thing your mother said to do and it worked for me."

"Nice save Dad."

"That's another thing you learn with time. When to kiss up," John whispers to him.

"Yeah, nice. We're going to have a little talk later John," Monica says to him.

Raina rolls over in bed and looks at her clock and its 4:10 PM. She reaches over, picks up the phone, and dials Sheena's number.

"Hey girl," Sheena hears Raina's hangover through her voice.

"Hey … what time is it?"

"After 4:00."

"I haven't gotten out of bed yet."

"Me too, I feel like crap."

"I'm never drinking like that again."

"It was those damn shots. I threw up twice this morning."

"Me too, I felt a little better after though."

"I gotta tell you something."

"What?"

"I kissed Dan last night."

Sheena sits up in her bed, "You what?! I'll be right over!"

The doorbell rings franticly and Raina opens her front door and sees Sheena standing there with a long coat and sunglasses. Sheena still has on underneath her overcoat her Hello Kitty pajamas and footies on. Raina looks at her and laughs.

"Damn, what did you do run here naked?"

"Whatever, you better give me the business."

Raina turns and walks upstairs to her room and Sheena follows her. Raina closes the door and then sits on the bed with Sheena.

"So, what happen?" Sheena eagerly asks.

"Well, he was helping me to the door, and I slipped and we were face to face and I don't know what came over me but I kissed him."

"Yes," Sheena exclaims.

"This isn't funny Sheena," Raina says mortified.

"Girl calm down it's not even that serious. You're acting as if something's wrong, you two are perfect for each other."

"Sheena, I've never kissed any guy who was involved with another woman, even though I don't like Lissa, I still wouldn't do her like that. I don't want Dan to get the wrong idea."

"I think you're over reacting a little bit. You were drunk, he was tipsy, he'll understand."

"You think so?"

"Yeah but even though you were drunk, that Bacardi brought something out of you that you wanted to do anyway."

"There you go again on that shit."

"So how was it?" Sheena asks.

"It was good his lips are so soft. I had butterflies in my stomach; I couldn't stop thinking about it."

"So if Lissa wasn't in the picture?"

"I don't know if I'm ready for that."

"Are you still in contact with Rashad?"

"He wrote me a letter last week and I don't know if I can write him back."

"Why?"

"He lied to me. He told me was gonna stop selling but he did it behind my back. I loved him so much and he lied to my face."

"Do you still love him?"

Raina shrugs her shoulders, "I don't know, I wanna be there for him cause I know he would lose it in there by himself. I just don't wanna give him the wrong idea about us getting back together."

"Well, Dan's a good guy even if his taste in woman is

questionable; he's really a sweet guy."

"I know, I just don't know what I'm gonna say to him."

♥♥♥

Monday morning at school after the weekend Dan is walking with Lissa through the food court. She looks at Dan, "You never called me this weekend Dan."

"I did on Saturday but you never picked up." Dan says to her.

"What time?" she asks.

"About 3:15"

"Oh, I was at the mall with Tamara."

"See I told you."

"Alright, so are you gonna come by my house this afternoon?" Lissa asks seductively.

"I would but I gotta stay after school and work with my staff writers on the newspaper."

She rolls her eyes, "Great."

"But I'll call you later okay?"

"Fine," Dan kisses her and Lissa walks down the hall to her first period class. Dan continues to walk to his class and sees Raina wearing some tight blue jeans that accents her curvy apple bottom ass. Raina opens her locker and puts her books inside her locker and Dan walks up to her.

"Hey?"

"Hey," Raina says shyly.

An awkward silence comes over them both.

"Are you feeling better?"

"Yeah, I was tore up on Saturday but I'm good now."

"That's good, who knew UNO could be so serious?"

"Yeah … Dan about what happen Friday night, I didn't mean to kiss you," Raina says embarrassed.

"Oh, that, we were both a little drunk, you more then me but it was like a reflex reaction or something," Dan says jokingly. "Don't even worry about it. It didn't mean anything did it?"

"No … of course not, picture you and me," Raina says lightheartedly.

"Yeah that's crazy."

"Yeah."

"So were cool?" Dan asks.

"Yeah, no doubt."

Raina playfully hits Dan in the shoulder. Standing away from a distance, Lissa sees them together. Lissa sees the chemistry between them and knows she can't allow this to continue.

The bell rings and everybody is walking outside of the school. Raina is walking out after school. Lissa walks up to her.

"Hi, uh, Rain right?" Lissa deliberately mispronounces.

"Raina," She corrects her.

"Whatever, I'm not going to beat around the bush, I don't like the way you've been all over Dan."

"What? All over him?"

Sheena sees Lissa in Raina's face and walks up to them.

"I don't know how you do things where you come from, but we don't get down like that here."

"What's going on? Sheena asks Raina.

"I don't know what you think you saw, but me and Dan are just friends."

"Yeah right, just remember who I am bitch," Lissa turns and walks away.

"What the hell was that all about?" Sheena yells.

"She was just marking her territory. This is exactly what I wanted to avoid."

"Well, let's go make some marks up side her head," Sheena yells.

"It's alright, I don't got time for her. Come on let's go."

Chapter 5

Like a Virgin- December 4th 1994

There are a few special days in a boy's life: when he gets his driver's license; when he scores the winning point in the game; and when he loses his virginity. Today is a special day for Dan. It's his eighteenth birthday, the day he becomes a man. And to celebrate this special occasion Dan's parents have rented out The Crush, a local teen club in Clearwater to throw him a party.

About 9:30pm Dan drives over to Lissa house to pick her up for the party. Dan is looking pretty fly wearing a Nautical Polo shirt and black slacks. He rings her doorbell and leans coolly against the door.

"Hey baby," Lisa answers.

"Hey ya self," Dan replies slowly seeing that Lissa is still in her robe. "You're not ready yet?"

Lissa opens the door and lets Dan enter.

"Oh, I'll be ready in a second," she tells him nonchalantly, ruffling her hair with her hands. Lissa looked like the actresses Jada Pinkett, with the attitude to match, just younger.

"Come on Lissa, the party starts at ten o'clock sharp. I can't be late for my own party."

"Of course you can. What are they gonna do start the party without you? Besides I gotta give you my gift first." Lisa takes Dan by the hand and walks him to her bedroom and closes the door.

"C'mon Lissa," Dan sighed and sat on her bed. "Can't you just give it to me later?" He looks at his watch, then back at Lissa as she admires herself in the mirror. Dan noticed that her dress was hanging on the door.

"No I can't." Lisa turns and faces Dan. "I've been thinking about this for a while now and I wanted to give you something nobody else has ever given you before."

Lissa pulls the tie on her robe and allows it to fall open, showing Dan her soft, curvy, and naked body. Her golden brown breasts were round and her nipples were erect. Her stomach was flat and she was freshly shaven between her thick thighs.

"Oh my ... wow," Dan utters softly. Lissa lets the robe drop to the floor and walks over to him.

"You're the first man to ever get this from me." She unzips his slacks and finds his rock hard penis and pulls it out. Her words to Dan confuses him because they've already have had sex before. Then he realizes what she means when he feels her warm moist mouth sliding down his penis. Dan moans as Lissa slowly bobs her head up and down his long shaft. She was right. This was a gift nobody else could have given him on this special night—his 18th birthday. In fact, it was his very first time getting oral sex. Lissa grasp the base of his penis and rubbed it up and down as she sucked him harder and made her mouth wetter. Dan's eyes rolled into the back of his head as he watched Lissa on her knees, between his legs, giving him the sweetest sensation he's ever felt. Finally after ten minutes Lissa let him slide out of her mouth and gave the tip a kiss. Dan fell back against the bed in bliss.

By the time he got cool, calm, and collected enough to sit up Lissa was already dress and ready to go.

"Come on baby you don't wanna be too late now do you?" Lissa teases.

"No ... that was one hell of a gift," Dan says to her delightfully.

She walks over to him sitting on the bed, "It was only for you baby, just remember that nobody else is gonna do you like me." Lissa gives him a long deep French kiss.

♥♥♥

Meanwhile at The Crush teen club, Raina, Sheena, Marcus and Cory are there with a couple of other of Dan's school friends enjoying the music. The DJ spins Da Brat's "Give It 2 Ya - Remix." Dan's mom and dad are waiting for him too.

"Where's Dan at? It's 10:25," Sheena asks Marcus.

"When I talk to him he said he was on his way to pick Lissa up from her house."

"Great," Sheena bleakly replies.

Raina felt the same way inside about seeing Lissa. Since their little confrontation after school that day, Raina has tired to keep her distance from Dan. Not because she's scared of Lissa because if she wanted to she could have kicked her ass. Raina feels like she has been through enough drama with Rashad and his ex-girlfriend to last her a lifetime. Sheena convinced her that this birthday party would be good and that Dan would love to see her. Raina wore a stunning sapphire dress fitting at the bust and hip with black open toe high heels. Cory couldn't believe how fine she looked tonight with her hair up and only a little make-up. Dan and Lissa made their grand entrance into the party and got hugs from his friends.

"Glad to see you could make it to your own party son."

"That's my fault Mr. Kelly. I had him begging me to hurry up and come," Lissa insinuates.

John looks at Dan strangely.

"Yeah Dad, you know how women can just have you waiting forever?"

"Yeah ... I do," John says suspiciously.

Dan sees Raina standing over at the other side with Sheena and Marcus and is breathless by how good she looks.

"Hey let's go over there," Dan says to Lissa.

"Hey what's up?"

"Happy Birthday Dan," Sheena says to him and gives

him a hug.

"What's up Dawg? Ya looking kinda GQ tonight," Marcus says to him.

"You know how I do."

"What's up man?" Cory gives Dan some dap.

"Happy Birthday Dan," Raina says.

He smiles, "Thank you Raina."

Lissa stares at Raina and rolls her eyes.

"Well I see you went to a store and picked up something to wear tonight. What was it a clearance sale?" Lissa asks snobbishly. Raina gets ready to fire back at her and Dan intervenes.

"Not tonight Lissa," Dan warns her.

"I was just given her some props," Lissa says flippantly.

"Well keep that backhanded shit to yourself," Sheena snaps at her.

"How about we get something to drink?" Dan quickly says to Lissa.

"Fine," Lissa replies looking Sheena up and down.

Dan and Lissa go to the bar and get themselves a soda.

"Never mind that bitch Raina," Sheena says to her.

"She got one more time to try me," Raina utters feeling her blood pleasure rise.

For the rest of the night Lissa is glued to Dan's hip until she has to use the bathroom. Dan was relived for the break. He spots Raina sitting at a table eating some cake and walks over toward her. *She looks so good... Perfect,* he thought to himself.

"Hey you."

"Hey birthday boy, you enjoying the party?"

"Yeah my folks went all out tonight. Hey listen about earlier I'm sorry about Lissa and her mouth. She …"

"It's okay Dan. I didn't come here tonight to see her. I came here tonight for you."

"Thanks. You look incredible tonight in that dress."

She blushes, "Thank you Dan."

Raina sees Lissa coming out of the ladies room.

"Well you better go get your girl before she sees you over here with me."

Dan sighs, "I'll talk to you later okay?"

"That's fine."

Later on Dan starts opening his gifts. He opens a box and sees that it's a Sony CD Walkman player from his mom and dad.

"Thanks Mom," Dan says to her and kisses her cheek.

"Thank your Dad, he's the one that picked it out."

"Of course, good looking out Dad."

"That's how I do it. Enjoy son."

Dan then sees a small box and picks it up and reads the card attach.

"Happy B-Day, I hope this satisfied your fetish, Raina," Dan looks at her smiles. Lissa glares at her.

"What does she mean by fetish?" Lissa whispers to Dan but he ignores her and opens the box. Whatever it is Lissa knows it can't compare to what she gave Dan earlier tonight. Dan sees a collection of three books by Donald Goines and his face lights up.

"Ha! Thank you Raina. I love Donald Goines! I haven't read these books yet."

"Enjoy them."

Lissa is pissed by how happy Dan is over some stupid books.

"Who the hell is Donald Goines?"

After the party Marcus drives Sheena home. Once again her father is spending the night at his girlfriend's house in Tampa. Sheena, being the responsible girl does what any girl in her situation would do. She invites Marcus in. They sit on the couch watching TV and Sheena looks over at Marcus. Marcus leans over and kisses her passionately. The sexual tension between them has been building like a snowball rolling down hill for months now. Before this, all they've done is some light petting but tonight was on a whole new level.

Marcus kisses her neck down to her soft brown shoulders. Sheena caresses Marcus's leg, then finds his growing manhood in his slacks and feels how hard he is. The excitement of touching Marcus makes her moist and her nipples become hard. Marcus pulls the strap of her party dress over her shoulders and her dress slides down and exposes her left breast. Marcus stares at her round succulent nipple and her big dark areola and grows even more aroused. He looks up at Sheena and she smiles at him. Marcus then kisses her nipple then begins to suck on it like an infant. Sheena has never been this horny before and unzips his pants and plays with Marcus now fully erect penis. Marcus hands also finds her moistness between her legs and begins to fondle her. As arousing and hot Sheena has become she still has doubts about going all the way yet.

"Marcus ... Marcus?"

"Yeah."

"Slow down."

"What?" Marcus eases up off of her.

"We can't do this yet."

"Oh ... I forgot. I got a condom in my wallet."

"No, that's not what I mean. I mean ... I got something I should tell you."

"What is it? What's wrong?"

"Marcus, I'm a ... I'm a virgin," Sheena says nervously.

"Excuse me," Marcus asks in shock. Sheena nods her head, "Why didn't you tell me this before?"

"I don't know. I thought you would find somebody else that would give you some."

Marcus smiles, "Sheena you're the one I wanna be with, the only one. So ... do you plan on waiting for marriage or something?" Marcus asks scared.

"Oh hell no!"

"Whew," Marcus breathes a breath of relief.

"I just want it to be a little bit more special then my

Dad's gone so let's get busy on the couch kinda thing," she quips.

Marcus laughs, "Okay. I'll make it special for you."

"I'm sorry I got you all worked up for nothing," Sheena regrettably says to him. "Don't worry about it. Its just gonna be another cold shower for me tonight."

"You do that too?!"

"Hell yeah, how do you think I've been able to get through theses past five months with you?"

Sheena smiles at him, "Well you don't have to go take that shower yet," Sheena says and pulls Marcus down on top of her. They continue their little grope fest with each other.

Chapter 6

Just Trying To Hook You Up -
December 19th 1994

Tonya is cooking dinner and Martin walks up behind her and kisses her neck. As of late, things have been strain between them with Martin's long hours at the hospital and Tonya working in a new firm. This is one of the rare evenings they were home together.

"Hey, what ya doing?" Tonya asks playfully.

"Checking your neck for soft spots, I think I'm going to have to give you a full body exam." Martin says to her.

"It's been a while since I had a check up."

"Well, later on you can step in my office and I can give you a complete work over."

"I can use an oral exam too doctor," Tonya says passionately.

Raina walks in and sees them getting frisky with each other.

"Oh my god, are you guys playing doctor again? I told you two not while I'm here. Last thing I need is to see you two bumping uglies." Raina says mortified.

"Then you better keep your eyes closed. Mama needs a check up." Tonya says to her.

"Oh yuck, be easy stomach," Raina grabs her belly and covers her mouth.

"Sorry honey, how is that project coming along?" Martin asks Raina.

"Oh, I'm almost done, matter of fact I was about to go over to Sheena's house to work on it. So you two can do whatever, my virgin eyes can't look at that kinda stuff."

"Virgin eyes, whatever, are you going to eat dinner before you go?" Tonya asks.

"Just keep it on the stove I'll get some later, see ya."

Raina walks out the door. Martin holds Tonya around her waist and grasps her passionately.

"Now where was I? oh yeah, I was about to give you a once over." Martin declares as he squeezes her breast.

"Once, I was hoping for twice or something."

Tonya says with a smile. Martin's beeper starts to buzz. Martin checks it.

"It's the hospital, I gotta take this."

He picks up the cordless phone and answers. Tonya becomes very frustrated by his call while Martin speaks on the cell phone to the hospital.

"Yes … I understand. I'll be there soon." Martin says and hangs up.

"I guess that check up will have to wait." Tonya says disappointed.

"I'm sorry baby it's an emergency."

"Isn't it always?" Tonya snaps annoyed.

"What's that suppose to mean?"

"We haven't seen much of each other lately."

"I'm on call baby, but I'll ask for some time off soon but for right now I gotta stay available."

"Martin, we haven't made love in over a two month and we're fighting almost every other day it seems. I don't know what's happing to us." Tonya says to him.

"I don't know. I … can't talk about this now. But when I get in we'll sit down and figure this out."

Martin grabs his jacket and walks out.

♥♥♥

Tyrone Mall is something like a home away form home for Sheena. To her, shopping should an Olympic sport. As ridiculous as it may sound when she breaks it down she has a good argument: One, you need to be quick on your feet to get to a sale. Two, you need plenty of stamina to go the four or five hours from store to store in pumps. Three, getting the best deal requires patience, comparing things and sometimes you need to be a good negotiator. Four, you have to be able to change into three or four different outfits lightening quick. Plus having your dad's American Express card doesn't hurt. Sheena and Raina are walking through the mall with shopping bags in hand.

"I love Bath and Body Works. I can't live without my cucumber melon lotion," Sheena says to Raina.

"Sweet pea is my thing."

"Plus, Marcus can't keep his lips off me when I put this on."

"Lips or tongue?"

"Yeah, that cucumber be so serious! Oh, let's go into Dillard's they got this Dooney & Bourke hand bag that would go perfect with this outfit I got last week." Sheena says.

"How much is it?"

"Oh, $179.00," Sheena says nonchalantly.

"I guess you gotta do what you gotta do to look good."

"As long as it looks good to me, it's worth it."

They see Dan, Marcus and Cory in Foot Locker. Dan looks so sexy to Raina as she remembers their kiss. Butterflies start to fill her stomach.

"There goes your man," Raina says to her.

"And he's here with your man, too."

"Shut up with that bullshit."

Raina pushes Sheena softly.

"Yeah you know it's true," Sheena says smiling at her. They walk over to them.

"What's up," Raina says to Dan.

"What's up stranger, you've been hiding out lately."

She arches her left eye, "Naw, you just need to open your eyes."

"What's up Raina?" Cory says.

"You remember my name, I'm impressed."

"Hey baby, what you about to get into?" Sheena says to Marcus.

"Hopefully you later." Marcus playfully confirms and Sheena starts to blush.

"Marcus! Stop that."

"Think I'm playing, oh, and you got the cucumber melon, it's over now," Marcus says as he pulls her close and kisses her neck.

"We'll see," She says with a devilish smile on her face. Marcus looks at Raina and laughs still recalling their UNO game.

"Hey, what's up *Draw Four?*" he says to her. They all laugh and Raina is annoyed by his humor.

"Oh, will you please die already," Raina says to Marcus.

"Hey, Raina can I talk to you for a second?" Cory asks.

"Yeah."

They step outside of the Foot Locker to talk and Dan looks concern. Cory gathers his thoughts as he looks at Raina's beautiful face. It was game time.

"First off, I wanna say sorry for calling you Rainy."

"Cory, that was months ago, you don't have to apologize for that, you didn't know."

"Well, I should have been more sensitive. Listen, I know you said it wasn't a big deal but I'd like to make it up to you. So, would you let me take you out tonight? I promise I'll be on my best behavior," Cory says with puppy dog eyes.

"Uh, okay."

"Really? Cool." Cory says surprised.

They walk back inside the store and Cory's behind Raina making faces to Marcus and Dan as if he is the man. Dan shakes his head in annoyance.

"Hey baby, we're gonna hit a few more stores before we go," Sheena says to Marcus. "So, you gonna come through to the crib later?"

"Yeah, I'll be there."

"Put that cream on too, okay," Marcus says.

"If you insist."

"See ya later." Raina says to Dan.

"Yeah, later."

Their tone to each other is as if they want to say more.

"I'll call you later," Cory says.

"Alright."

Sheena and Raina walk out of Foot Locker and down to the other store.

"You two are going out tonight? Why?"

"He asked so I figure why not? I might as well have some fun."

"What about Dan?" Sheena asks her.

"He's got a girlfriend."

Cory walks back inside of the Foot Locker with a shit-eating grin on his face. The guys are standing by the shoe rack. Dan not wanting to show his anger at Cory talking to Raina turns and picks up a pair of Nikes off the shelf.

"I told you I was gonna pull Cleveland dawg," Cory says to them.

"I guess so." Marcus says to him.

Cory picks up his shoebox and walks to front counter, "Let me go pay for these." Cory walks to the resister.

"You all right man," Marcus asks Dan.

"Yeah I'm cool."

Cory and Raina are parked alone at Gulf Port beach, his spot where he's brought plenty of girls. Raina has on a sleeveless shirt and jeans and Cory wearing an Orlando Magic Shaq jersey. He's playing Intro's "Come Inside" on the cassette radio. "I love this song." He says as he sings along with the group.

"Yeah, I like it too." Cory starts to sing along with the

song off key. Raina grimaces and tries to look the other way.

"I love coming here."

"Really?" Raina says suspiciously.

"Yeah, I come here all the time and look at the water and stars;it's beautiful. Not as beautiful as you though."

"So I'm the first girl you've brought up here right?"

"Oh yeah, no doubt, I don't like to show this side of me to just anybody. But there's just something about you, you're just so damn fine. Ever since I first saw you I knew I had to be with you."

Cory pulls closer and starts to kiss on her neck. Raina rolls her eyes and turns her face away from him to avoid face contact. He puts her hand on his member.

"Hey, what're you doing?"

"You don't know what you do to me," Cory moans out.

"I know what you doing to my hand!" She pulls her hand way.

"I'm sorry I can't help it. I just want you so bad."

"Cory, I'm not gonna sleep with you."

"We don't have to do that, you don't have to do nothing to me. Just let me eat you out." Cory begs. It takes Raina a second to register what he's just said to her. She doesn't know weather to laugh or throw up.

"What? Nigga get the hell off me! I can't believe you just tried me like that! Take me home!" Raina demands.

"Hey, why you getting so up tight, I'm just trying to hook you up," Cory says confused by her reaction.

"Fool, I ain't trying to hook up to you in any kind of way! Take me home damn it!!"

"Aight, alright just calm down!"

"Now! I can't believe this shit!"

♥ ♥ ♥

Raina comes in after her date with Cory, tosses her bag on the chair, picks up her phone, and calls Sheena. Sheena picks up her phone while doing her nails on top of her bed.

She continues to paint her toes candy apple red while holding the phone to her ear with her shoulders.

"Hello," Sheena answers.

"What's up girl," Raina says to her.

"Hey … what's wrong you sound upset?"

"You won't believe what happened to me."

"What, what happened?"

"Cory happened," Raina yells.

"Didn't I warn you about him? What did he do?" Sheena asks already knowing what Cory is known for trying with some other girls.

"This fool wanted to eat me out!" Raina yells.

"What! Oh my god!! Did he try to?"

"Hell yeah," Raina replies.

Sheena bursts out laughing hysterically.

"That ain't funny!" But Raina starts to laugh too.

Sheena still not able to stop laughing says to her jokingly, "So, did you let him taste it?"

"Hell naw," Raina yells disgusted.

"I'm sorry girl, but this is too funny," Sheena says as her stomach starts to hurt from laughing too hard.

"I can't believe he tried me like that."

"I knew Cory was grimy but didn't think he would do it like that! Hey, we're still getting together tomorrow night?"

"Yeah."

"Don't worry girl I got away to get back at him."

"Cool."

Chapter 7

Truth or Dare- December 20ᵗʰ 1994

The next night at Sheena's house, Raina is setting up things for the guys. Raina looks at Sheena pouring what looks like some trail mix into a bowl.

"So, your dad is cool with letting you have people over like this all the time?" Raina asks her.

"My dad went to Miami for the weekend with his girlfriend; something about wanting to keep their relationship fresh and new," Sheena says.

"That's good right?"

"Chances are they're in a hotel down there getting their freak on."

"Oh god, I almost walked in on my parents the other day. I'm not trying to have that mental picture burn into my brain," Raina says relieved.

"Girl, my dad is a freak, I've seen things no kid should see," Sheena laughs.

"Must be where I get it from!"

Two cars pull up to the house. Marcus and Dan get out of his Probe and Cory get out of Dodge Neon.

"I thought Lissa was coming too." Marcus asks Dan.

"She said she had to study tonight," Dan tells him.

"Again?"

"I know, she ain't the social type."

"Or the football type, party type, be around your friends type …" Marcus says and Dan laughs.

"Where the hoes at?" Cory asks.

"You still ain't tell us about last night with Raina," Dan asks him.

"Yeah man what's up?" Marcus asks Cory.

"Yo, she was all on me," Cory says proudly. "I took her to the spot put on some Intro and it was on."

"Really?" Dan asks surprised at what he says.

"Yeah I had to break her off. She can take a stiff one for sure," Cory pauses as another car pulls up in front of Sheena's house and two sexy girls get out of the other car. "Oh, damn Sheena got some fine ass friends dawg."

A gorgeous Puerto Rican girl named Yaritza Lopez and a sexy coffee brown skinned Catriona Miles walk to the house. Yaritza wearing a red fitted Nautica sweater that hugs her well-endowed breasts, tight blue jeans, and white and blue Reeboks. Catriona wore a short red flannel skirt that barely covered her voluptuous butt, a tight white long sleeved tee, and black high heels. Cory mouth hangs open as he stares at the sexy pair walk to the front door. It was time to *kick game* he thought.

"There her friends from last year, I think they go to SPJC now," Marcus tells him.

"Let me go introduce myself," Cory says cockily. The guys follow the girls into Sheena's house. The girls are in the living room talking to each other. Raina feels a little awkward meeting Sheena's old friends for some reason.

"Raina, these are my girls, Yaritza and Catriona." Sheena says to her.

"Hey, what's up?" Yaritza says.

"Hey, how you doing?" Catriona says.

"I' m good," Raina replies.

"So you have been dealing with Sheena, huh?" Catriona asks her.

"What … shut up girl. You make it sound like I'm a bad influence or something," Sheena says to her.

"I'm just saying, the poor girl doesn't know what she gotten into with you." Catriona says.

"Oh my god!"

"Has she made you play Drinking UNO yet?" Yaritza asks Raina.

"Yeah, never again," Raina says to her.

"See what I mean? She's a wicked little thing," Catriona says.

"Fo sho," Raina says laughing.

"You know what, forget all of y'all. How ya like that?" Sheena says sarcastically.

Cory, Dan, and Marcus come in the living room.

"What's up ladies, how y'all … doing?" Cory sees Raina sitting on the couch, she cuts her eyes at him. Cory doesn't speak to her.

"Hey sexy, what's up y'all?" Marcus says.

"Hey baby," Sheena kisses him.

"What's up," Dan says to them. Raina sees Dan and smiles at him but he doesn't know if what Cory said was true or not.

"Okay y'all let's get this started," Sheena says.

"Okay, what is it this time? Drinking Checkers, Three Shots Poker, what?" Dan asks her.

"No, we're just going to play a little game of Truth or Dare," Sheena says casually.

"Oh, okay."

"If you don't tell the truth, you gotta take a shot of this …" Sheena takes out a bottle of Vodka and a bottle of Coke.

"Vodka and Coke, oh lord," Raina says.

"This is exactly what I mean girl," Catriona says to Raina.

"That's right, it gets even better if you don't do the dare you get to eat a nice doggy treat." Sheena holds out a bowl of Kibbles & Bits.

Raina gets up and pulls Sheena into the other room.

"Girl I can't go home drunk again or my dad will kill me."

"That's why I got the Coke. We got messed up last time because we were taking it straight from the bottle. Trust me the dares are not that bad."

"That idiot Cory's here though."

"Just like I planned. Trust me I got his number. But hey, Dan's here too," Sheena mentions and Raina smiles. They walk back into the living room.

"Okay, this is how the game goes; all the cards are placed in a bowl and we pick a card. We'll draw numbers to see who goes first," Sheena explains.

They draw numbers and Yaritza pulls the highest number and picks first.

"I swear Sheena if this is bad, I'll kick your ass."

"Just read it."

"Truth, have you ever had mercy sex?" She reads out loud.

"What the hell is mercy sex?" Dan asks.

"It's when you have sex with somebody you normally wouldn't be caught dead with out in public. Tell the truth Yaritza," Sheena says to her.

"I can't believe I'm about to say this. Oh god, okay yes, I didn't see him again after that, I just really needed some that night. Okay," Yaritza says.

"Can you have a little mercy on me?" Dan says laughing.

"Shut up!" Yaritza yells, "Your go Sheena."

Sheena pulls a card from the bowl. *"Truth, when was the last time you had sex? And with who?"* Sheena reads the card and looks at Marcus.

"Come on Sheena tell the truth," Yaritza says to her.

"I plead the fifth," Sheena says and pours out some Vodka and a little Coke and drinks a glass. "Aaahhh, refreshing!"

"You chicken! I bet you're freaking poor Marcus to death!" Yaritza exclaims. Sheena smiles and looks at Marcus.

"Your go Raina."

"Dare, tongue kiss someone of the opposite sex. Damn, why me?" Raina yells.

"Oh girl, you better make it a wet one," Raina glares at Cory and then grabs Dan's hand. "Come on."

She gives Dan a big open mouth kiss that lasts for about ten seconds. Raina purposely draws out the kiss because it's Dan but also to mess with Cory.

"Damn ... you go girl," Sheena yells.

"Thank you for the lip service," Raina says to Dan.

"Anytime," He says to her with a smile.

Cory pulls a card and reads it. *"Truth, have you ever begged for sex?* Hell naw, never."

"Is that true Raina," Sheena asks her. Raina smiles and looks at Cory and he gets a panicky expression on his face.

"I coulda swore he was Keith Sweat last night," Raina says and looks at Cory. Dan shakes his head and laughs.

"Oh damn dog! I hope you got room for a snack," Marcus says laughing.

"Oh hell naw, I ain't doing that shit!" Cory yells.

"So you gonna punk out?" Dan yells.

"I'm not eating that shit man. She's lying," Cory says to them.

"I'm lying? I bet you told everybody you screwed me last night didn't you? You sorry ass ... did you tell them you were begging me to eat me out!"

"You lying ass nigga you told me and Marcus she was all over you," Dan yells at him. Cory looks at the girls and is as embarrassed as hell.

"So why don't you tell me how good you put it on me," Raina asks him.

"Alright, so I exaggerated the truth a little. Happy? I'll take a bit of it, if that's what y'all want so bad," Cory eats the dog cracker.

"Oh shit!" Marcus yells.

"Eat up." Raina says to him. The taste is so nasty he spits it out.

Cory's face grimaces, "I can't do it!"

"That's what you get for lying on me."

Cory spits the dog cracker into the garbage can.

"Damn, she put you on blast," Marcus says laughing. Everybody is laughing at him.

"Drink up punk," Raina snaps at him and gives him the Vodka and Coke and Cory drinks a whole cup. Dan picks a card from the bowl.

"Dare, show your underwear to everybody"

"Oh, this should be good," Catriona says.

"Take it off," Raina says to him.

"Show us what you're working with!" Sheena yells.

"Hey, Marc, Cory turn y'all heads man!"

"You don't even have to ask," Marcus says discussed. Dan pulls his pants down and shows his white boxer briefs to the girls. Raina looks shock at the package he has imprinted.

"No wonder Lissa so sprung," Raina whispers to Sheena. Dan pulls his pants up and shakes his head.

"Truth, when was the last time you gave oral sex?" Marcus reads.

"Ah, pass me the Vodka please," Marcus requests and everybody looks at Sheena and she starts to blush uncontrollability.

"What da bumbaclot? You two are so freaky! You and me are gonna talk later Sheena!" Catriona yells.

"Anyway, I don't know what you're talking about! It's your go Raina," Sheena says to her. Raina pulls a card from the bowl and reads it.

"Let's see what crazy thing I gotta do this time. *Dare, give someone a lap dance.*" All I gotta say is why me? Damn Sheena!"

"I got your back girl," Sheena says laughing. Sheena turns Jodeci's "Feenin'" on the stereo. There you go girl!

"I'm gonna get you back for this I swear."

"Well you can always drink some Vodka or eat some Kibbles & Bits," Sheena says sarcastically. Raina knows she isn't going to drink after how sick she got last time.

"Here you go, just back it up right here," Cory pats his lap.

"Negro please! Do you mind?" Raina asks Dan.

"Naw, go ahead. Do what ya gotta do."

Dan looks over at Cory and laughs. Raina starts to dance in front of Dan and slowly comes down on his crotch. She starts to grind on him slowly and is enjoying it just as much as he is. Raina is starting to feel the huge package of Dan's growing harder through his pants and whines on him harder. Until she starts to get a little to hot herself then she gets off of him.

"You alright D?" Marcus asks.

"Oh yeah. Just give me a second."

Dan pulls a card and reads it. *Truth, what's the difference between having sex and making love?"* Dan pauses for a second and gathers his thoughts. "I guess, you could really have sex with anybody and not emotionally care for them. Making love involves feelings, I mean, you really care more about what the other person feels then yourself."

Catriona pulls a card from the bowl. *"Dare, let somebody kiss both of your nipples or eat Kibbles & Bits."* Oh hell no! You're such a dirty little girl Sheena," Catriona yells.

"I told you I'd get the last laugh. So, do you like your Kibbles with cheese?" Sheena says laughing.

"Oh god …" Catriona looks at Cory. "Hey you come here." Cory eyes light up and stares at Catriona's 35C breast. Catriona wore a tight white long sleeved tee with no bra tonight.

"Yeah," Cory yells and leaps across the coffee table to her.

"Okay do it through my shirt," Catriona says to him.

"What?"

"Chicken shit!" Sheena yells at her.

"You didn't say I had to take my shirt off. Well come on, do you want to or not?" Catriona asks him. Cory face flies into her breast and he kisses both nipples for three seconds each leaving a wet spots on her shirt. Catriona shakes her head then takes a gulp of her drink.

"Damn Cory got milk?" Marcus asks.

Yaritza reads a card, *"Truth, when was the last time you masturbated?"*

"Oh hell naw," Catriona says laughing.

"Why do I keep on getting these jacked up questions," Yaritza yells.

"You're just luckily I guess." Marcus says.

Yaritza shakes her head.

"Somebody give me the damn Vodka I ain't answering

that shit!" She yells.

"Can I smell your fingers," Dan asks Yaritza jokingly.

"Ew, you nasty thing!" Raina yells at him and he grins.

"Truth, what's the difference between being in love and having love for someone?" Raina reads. "How I'm I supposed to answer that?"

"From the heart," Sheena says to her.

"I think having love somebody is like showing affection for somebody or doing things for them. Being in love goes deeper, it's like you care more about their happiness then yours."

"Okay, you two are way too deep for your own good," Marcus says to them.

"Damn, this is better then Oprah," Catriona says.

After they got done playing, Catriona and Yaritza were walking to their car. Cory decides it's time to put his game down on Catriona's fine ass. Like a true pimp Cory is unfazed by the embarrassment he suffered earlier tonight. Either he was a true playa or a horny fool that doesn't no the meaning of the word quit.

"Hey shorty hold up," Cory says to Catriona and she turns around.

"You talking to me?"

"Yeah, listen I know there were a lot of things said in there to mess with me but I was really feeling the vibe between you and me in there."

"You were?" Catriona says with reservations.

"Yeah so I was wondering can I give you a call and we can talk sometime, ya'know? So we can really get to know each other."

"Baby boy, if you have to beg for sex, you're not ready for me. I would turn your little skinny behind out," Catriona says as she gets in the car with Yaritza and they start to laugh, then they pull off.

"I'm willing to learn," Cory yells.

Raina walks with Dan to his car.

"That was very deep what you said in there," Dan says to her.

"I guess I've been in love a few times to know the difference."

"That's a good thing."

"So did you get a chance to read your books?" she asks.

"Yeah I finished *Black Gangster*. Oh, and I got a book for you too."

"Which one?"

"*Waiting to Exhale*."

"Good, I haven't read that yet."

"Do you wanna stop by my house and get it?" Dan asks timidly.

"Sure."

♥♥♥

Dan and Raina ride in his Probe to his house a few blocks away. When they walk in the front door they see Dan's parents watching TV. Monica sees Raina and knows this is the girl he's been talking to them about and remembers her from the party.

"Hey Mom and Dad, this is Raina," Dan introduces her.

"Hello, we meet at Dan's birthday party. You're the one that got him the books." Monica says to her.

"Yeah, I didn't know what to get him really. I just knew he likes books just like me so it was just easy to get him some books," Raina says to her.

"Oh, I think it takes a lot more then just dumb luck to get a really thoughtful gift like that for him. And I loved that dress you had on too," Monica says to her.

"Thanks, my mom helped me pick it out for me."

Dan looks at them talking to each other like old friends. His mom and Lissa never talked to each other like this.

"Well, we came by to pick up a book."

"Well, it was nice to see you again Raina. Don't be a stranger," Monica says.

"Thank you Mrs. Kelly."

John stands up and greets her, "Hi, nice to finally meet you."

"Hello … finally meet me," Raina asks confused by his words. Dan didn't want Raina to know that he's been talking about her to them.

"My dad meant it's nice to finally meet one of my friends."

"Yeah that's what I meant."

"I'm gonna give Raina that book now," Dan says trying to get out of this awkward moment.

"Nice to meet you both." Raina says to them.

"You too." Monica says to her. They walk to his room.

"I like her already. I hope he doesn't let her slip away." Monica says to John.

"He'll do the right thing. Just give him time."

Dan takes Raina into his room and she sits in the chair at his desk. "Do you want something to drink?"

"Naw, I'm good. Listen, about earlier, I didn't mean to put you on the spot like that. It's just with Cory there …"

"Say no more. It's all good."

"I mean, I know you and Lissa are kicking it," Raina says to him.

"Hey, you don't tell I won't. Cory told us you were sprung off of him."

She frowns, "Hell no, your little friend is a pervert."

"I should have known he was lying."

"Trying to make me look like a hoe," Raina says pissed.

"Well other than your close encounter, how do you like it down here so far?"

"It's alright, it's different but there's some things I really do like down here," Raina says smiling at him.

"I feel ya."

Raina looks at Dan's desktop, "What's that?"

Raina sees a notebook with Dan's hand writing in it. She

picks it up.

"Oh, that's just a hobby I got. I like to write short stories."

Dan tries to down play it as Raina reads a few pages.

"Oh my god, this is good! No wonder you know so much about different authors. Well I guess I know what you'll be doing after high school."

"Well, me and Lissa talk about it and she thinks law school would be a little more profitable in the long run."

"But will you be happy?"

He shrugs his shoulders, "I don't know."

"Has she read your stuff?" Raina asks him concerned.

"Yeah, well, not all of it, she just thinks I should focus more on our future together."

"Dan, I've just read a couple of pages here and I can tell you have a gift. You can't let that go to waste," Raina says sincerely.

"You really like it?"

"Hell yeah! I wouldn't say it if I didn't think so. Dan you gotta ask yourself what do you really want to do with your life."

"How come you're so concerned about what I do?"

Raina pauses for a second as if she has said too much.

"I don't, I'm just thinking of my book collection. I'm gonna need something good to read in the future."

"Right, I'll keep that in mind," Dan says with a grin.

"Good," Raina replies nervously.

"Here's the book."

Dan hands her *Waiting to Exhale.*

"Thanks."

Chapter 8

🏹 Cupid Sucks- February 14th 1995

The second semester of school is in full swing and the Multicultural Club has organized a dance for Valentines Day. Sheena, Raina, and Marcus made sure everything is ready for Saturday the eighteenth. Since the truth or dare game back in December, Dan and Raina have been spending more time together talking about different books and she's been reading his stories.

Of course this has been done on the low so that Lissa doesn't flip out when she sees them together. Raina has been trying to figure out what she's been feeling for Dan and tells herself that they're just friends. A lie she hopes that not true deep down inside. But the more time she spends with him the deeper her feelings become for him. All of the drama she had back in Cleveland seems to feel like a lifetime ago. But the past always has a way of sneaking up on you, yesterday she from a letter from her ex-boyfriend Rashad in prison.

Dear Raina,

I hope you get this letter and that your aight. I heard you and your family moved to Florida a few months ago. I know I messed up things between us and I shouldn't have lied to you. Please don't hate me. Life in here is a livin' hell. The guards treat you like shit and the food *here is nasty. Everyday I sit in my cell and wish I could see you again. If I could take it all back I would but I know I can't un-break your heart.*

I know that you might have found someone else new in your life and I'm not mad at you. I just want you to be happy. All I want from you is your friendship again and to know that you can forgive me. That's the worst part about being in here is knowing that I hurt you. Please write me back and let me know how you're doing. You're my heart.

Love,

Rashad

Raina showed the letter to Sheena at school.

"Damn girl. He sounds so depressed in there," Sheena says to her.

"I know."

"Are you gonna write him back?"

"As much as he hurt me I can't let him suffer like that in there alone," Raina says to her as they sit in their English III class.

"That's good at least he won't hurt himself in there."

"Yeah, that's what I'm worried about," Raina says concern.

"Well on a happier note do you know who you're going with to the dance yet?"

"Nope. Mario asked me to go with him and so did Nassouri. But I know Mario is messing with Tequilla Greene so I ain't trying to get caught up in that shit. And Nassouri is cute but I think Cory and him are friends so they might be trying to see who can get in my pants first," Raina says turned off.

"Yeah Nassouri's a pretty boy. He's gonna be expecting some ass by the end of the night. He's already done ran up into half the girls on the cheerleading squad," Sheena says to her, "Besides I guess since Dan's not available you really don't want nobody else."

Raina looks at her and laughs, "Why do you always bringing him up?"

"You know why. After how freaky you two got at my house you can't tell me anything."

"NE-way! Like I was saying I don't got nobody to go with to the dance. Raina says firmly.

"Well you can always go solo with us."

"Thanks, I'm starting to feel like a third wheel around you two. I'm sure Marcus wants to spend some time alone with you."

"Oh Marcus will get his time. After what we talked about, he's gonna wait for me."

"That's good. Not too many dudes would stick around if a girl ain't giving it up."

Meanwhile in the gym basketball court Dan and Marcus are having a similar conversation.

"So are you gonna tell me what's going on with you two? Check."

Marcus bounces the basketball to Dan.

"What are you talking about?" Dan bounces the ball back to him.

"I mean you and Raina. You guys are spending a lot more time around each other."

"We like the same books." Dan says to him.

"Ain't that much book love in the world." Marcus jokes as he dribbles and backs Dan down into the paint.

"It's just refreshing having somebody I can talk to about my stuff." Marcus spins and shoots the ball and scores.

"True. But it's more then a book of the month thing with you two," Dan throws him the ball.

"Maybe."

"It's just I don't know what to do."

"Check." Dan throws Marcus the ball.

"I love being around Raina. She makes me feel good."

"And Lissa?"

"Well, she makes me feel real good too," Dan confirms and Marcus pulls up and takes a shot. The ball hits the rim and Dan rebounds the ball.

"Dawg, I didn't tell you this but you know why I was late coming to my birthday party?"

"Naw, why?"

"Lissa gave me her gift." Dan says as he gestures his hand down to his crotch.

"You mean she …"

"Yes she did and very well too. She had my toes curling."

"Yo, you know I don't like Lissa but she is fine. I'll give her that. And for her to give you the business like that means she's really feeling you."

Dan shoots a three pointer and makes it.

"Game. But then there's Raina and I can't explain it but I just feel attracted to her so much. And it's just not because she's fine as hell it's like … she gets me."

"Well my friend I can't tell you what you should do but you better make up your mind soon. Raina ain't gonna be single forever. Not the way these niggas around here be jocking her."

"Yeah I know," They both go sit on the bench.

"So what's up with Sheena?"

"Well I didn't tell you but after your party we went back to her place and things got heated."

"What? So did you …"

"No. Dawg, she's a virgin."

Dan's eyebrows arch, "Excuse me?"

"I know! I said the same thing too!"

"I mean I know Sheena ain't no hoe but I thought

somebody might of tap that by now."

"Nope. She told me she wants to but she doesn't wanna just rush into it." Marcus says to him.

"You know, I respect that. Not too many girls nowadays are saving the gift."

"I know, she's worth waiting for. I'm telling ya dawg, I know it might sound crazy but she could be the one someday," Marcus says seriously.

"Really? It's like that?"

"Man, when it's real. You don't even have to ask."

The Friday afternoon before the dance, Raina comes by Dan's house and sees his mom. Raina wore her long black hair in a ponytail today with a white tank top and jeans. Monica, Dan's mother opens the door and smiles seeing Raina. She secretly hoped that Dan shared more then a *friendship* with this beautiful young lady.

"Hey Mrs. Kelly, how you doing?" Raina asks her.

"I'm good Raina, you look nice today."

"Thank you, is Dan in his room?"

"Yeah I think he's still trying to figure out what suit he's going to wear to the dance. Have you picked out a dress yet?" Monica asks her.

"Well I don't think I'm gonna go."

"Why not? It sounds like fun," Monica asks concern.

"I don't have anybody to go with and the whole theme of the dance is cupid and couples. And seeing how I'm not a couple, I think I might skip this one."

"It's a shame. I think Dan would've like to see you there."

"Well he's got Lissa to occupy his time."

Monica rolls her eyes, "I hope you reconsider."

Dan comes out of his room and into the living room and sees Raina and his mom and over hears the last part of their conversation.

"You're not going?" he asks her.

"I haven't made up my mind yet."

Monica walks to the kitchen, "I'll let you two talk."

Dan walks up to her and Raina feels her heart skip.

"Well it'll be a shame considering how hard you and Sheena worked on it. You won't even be there to enjoy it."

"At least you will."

"Here's the book you wanted to read." Dan hands her the book and she touches his hand and they stare at each other. Just then Monica returns to the living room with Lissa.

"Dan, Lissa here to see you." Monica says.

Lissa is pissed to see Raina touching Dan's hand.

"Thanks," Raina says to him and takes the book.

"*Daniel* are you ready to take me to get a pair of shoes for my dress tomorrow night?" Lissa says in a raised tone.

"Yeah."

"Well I gotta go. Thanks for the book Dan," Raina says to him and starts to leave.

"So are you coming to the dance Raina?" Lissa asks her.

"Probably not."

"Couldn't find a date huh?" Lissa rudely implies.

Raina feels the hairs on the back of her neck raise but holds her tongue, "Something like that. See ya Dan. Bye Mrs. Kelly."

Raina says and walks out.

"Bye Raina," Monica says as she shakes her head and walks back into the kitchen.

"Why do you always have to say things like that to her?" Dan asks.

"Why? What is she even doing here Daniel?" Lissa snaps.

"She was borrowing a book."

"She can't get one from the library like everybody else?" Lissa spits.

"Don't start that."

"Fine. Can we go now?"

"Yeah," Dan says flippantly. Lissa turns and storms out of the door and Dan reluctantly follow her.

♥♥♥

That night Lakewood High's gym has been transformed into a Valentines Day love nest for the dance. Pink and red balloons are all around the gym and huge hand painted posters of cupid shooting his arrow hang on the walls. Dan and Lissa walk into the already crowed gym; Lissa is wearing an emerald strap dress while Dan wears a black rayon shirt and slacks. They walk over to Marcus and Sheena dancing near the DJ booth. Shai's 'Baby I'm Yours' is playing in the background.

"What's up y'all," Dan says to Sheena and Marcus.

"Hey Dan," Sheena says to him.

"What's up dawg?" Marcus gives him some dap.

"The gym looks nice Sheena," Lissa says to her.

"Thanks … Lissa."

Sheena is surprised she would say anything nice to her at all and so is Dan and Marcus.

"You're really good at manual labor," Lissa says mockingly.

Sheena doesn't know wheatear to thank her or slap her.

"Did she just say I'm good at-"

"We'll see you guys later," Dan says and quickly walks away with Lissa.

"Why do you always do that?" Dan asks her.

"Do what? I was just given her a complement."

"No, you were being rude."

"Whatever," Lissa turns and walks to the table behind them and gets some punch. Cory walks up to Dan with his date.

"What's up playboy?" Cory says.

"What's going on Cory?" Dan says and gives him some dap.

"Just chilling with my home girl Angela."

"It's Tangela," She corrects him.

"Yeah Tangela that's what I meant," Cory says to her. Tangela rolls her eyes. Dan looks towards the door and sees

Raina walk in wearing a dazzling low cut red spaghetti strap dress that stops half way down her thick luscious legs. She wore her hair down around her shoulders.

"Damn …" Dan utters softly. Cory turned around to see who he was looking at and sees Raina.

"Holy shit," Cory yells and Tangela cuts her eyes at him.

"You do know I'm standing right here don't ya," Tangela asks him.

Cory shrugs his shoulders, "Yeah … so?"

Raina walks in and spots Sheena and walks over toward her.

"Damn girl, so I guessed you changed your mind," Sheena says to her.

"Yeah I decided to pop in," Raina replies.

"Dan's over there with Lissa," Marcus mentions to her.

Raina looks over at them, "Really, I hope they have fun."

"You look good tonight girl," Sheena complements her.

"Thanks you do too."

Some guys walk by and stare at Raina.

"Looks like you ain't gonna have a hard time finding someone to dance with," Sheena says to her. Raina looks over and sees Dan staring at her from across the dance floor.

"I probably won't." Raina agrees. Dan walks over to Raina through the crowd.

He smiles, "Hey, you made it."

"Yeah, here I am," Raina replies happily.

"What made you change your mind?" Dan asks her.

"Your mother. She said I should come and enjoy myself so I decided to take her advice."

"I'm glad you did. You look great."

"Thanks, you don't look half bad yourself."

Lissa walks over and sees Dan talking to Raina.

"Well, well, well … look who decided to show up. Guess you found a date," Lissa spits to Raina.

"No, I'm here solo."

"Damn shame, let's dance Dan."

"Okay, I'll talk to you later," Dan says to Raina.

"That's fine."

Dan walks with Lissa to the dance floor and begin to slow dance to Keith Sweat and Athena Cage's 'Nobody'. Glen walks up to Raina and asks her to dance and she accepts. While dancing with Lissa, Dan catches eyes with Raina and they stare at each other then look away. After the song ends Lissa sees Tamara and she goes and talks to her. Dan walks over to Marcus and Sheena, while Raina continues to dance with Glen.

"Hey, Sheena I'm sorry for what Lissa said to you."

"Never mind." Sheena replies. "So did you all know Raina was coming tonight?" Dan asks them.

"Naw, but she did make a hell of an entrance. I think she only came for one reason," Marcus points out to him.

"Why?"

"Come on Dan, what do you think," Sheena blurts.

Lissa walks back over to Dan with Tamara, "Dan, Tamara told me that Carl Nixon is having a house party."

"Okay and," Dan replies suspicious of her motives.

"And I wanna go."

"We just got here and you're ready to go," Dan asks her confused.

"This dance is lame. I'm ready to go," Lissa demands.

Dan was annoyed by her attitude, "Well I'm not."

Narrowing her eyes on him and speaking through clench teeth, "*Daniel* I'm ready to go."

"If you wanna go, then go. I'm staying," Dan says to her firmly.

"Fine stay," Lissa spits angrily and then turns to Tamara "Come on girl!"

They turn and leave the dance.

"Whatever," Dan utters unfazed by her theatrics'.

"Whoa ... Now that was ill," Marcus quips.

"I'm just tired of her acting like that. It's always what she wants to do."

"Well now that she's gone you can have some fun," Sheena declares.

Dan laughs, "Well I guess you're right."

Dan looks over and spots Raina still dancing with Glen. She came here tonight for him. Dan thought to himself that maybe this was all happening for a reason.

"Damn girl, you look good tonight," Glen affirms while dancing with her. "Did you wear that dress tonight for me?"

Raina rolls her eyes, "I just threw something on Glen."

"Well I came her on my own tonight so why don't we just leave here together?" he suggests.

The song ends and Raina steps away.

"I'm just doing me right now," Raina informs him and walks away.

She cuts through the crowd and goes and gets some punch. As she drinks her punch she feels a tap on her shoulders.

"What do you want now Glen?" Raina turns around and sees Dan.

"Sorry wrong guy."

"Dan, sorry I thought you were … anyway what's up?"

"I was just wondering if you'd like to dance with me?"

Raina's heart skips a beat, "Dance with you? What about Lissa?"

"She left."

"Without you?" Raina asks surprised.

"Yeah, so do you wanna dance?" he holds out his hand.

She smiles, "Yeah."

The DJ is playing Tevin Campbell's 'I'm Ready'. Raina puts her head on Dan's shoulder and they slowly dance together on the dance floor. Dan holds her tightly around her waist. Her body felt so perfect against his. For the next few seconds everybody else fade away and it's just them holding each other. Once again Raina is staring into Dan's big brown eyes and Dan into hers. Dan slowly leans forward and kisses her lips tenderly. Although they have kissed before some how this was different. It wasn't a drunken accident or a dare playing a game. This was real. As their lips tug on each other and their soft tender kiss turns into a passionate

French kiss and Dan pulls her body closer to him. Raina folds her arms around his neck. All of their passion for each other has found a release. Raina then pulls away slowly as if she's disappointed in herself for allowing this to happen.

"I can't do this," Raina says and walks away.

"Do what? Raina? Raina?" Dan says as she walks away.

Marcus walks up to Dan. "Well, just don't stand there fool, go after her!"

Dan chases Raina outside the gym.

"Raina wait," She stops and turns around. "Why are you running away from me?"

"Dan, what are we doing? What've we been doing theses past few months?"

"Nothing, we're friends."

"Dan I've kissed you more times then any friend I've ever had in my life. I don't wanna be that other woman on the side."

"You're not," Dan insists.

"Dan, you got Lissa," Raina says regrettably.

"I know … but it's different with you then with her."

"You can't have us both Dan."

Raina turns and walks away while Dan stands frozen in his tracks.

Chapter 9

Love & War- March 22ⁿᵈ 1995

Since the Valentines dance Raina has kept her distance from Dan and he from her. Lissa and Dan made up a few days later but things have been strained at best between them. Lissa tried to make things better with sex, letting him have it with no condom most of the time. No matter how good the sex may be Dan can't help but feel there's something lacking in their relationship.

As the school year draws closer to the end everybody is applying for colleges and universities across the country. Even though Dan has been interested in becoming a lawyer since freshmen year his last two years as editor of the newspaper has really sparked his interest in writing although Lissa sees his writing as just a hobby. Dan has been looking at colleges for journalism even thought Lissa has been in his ear about law school.

Sooner or later Dan knows he's got to make a decision about what he wants to do with his life. He misses spending time with Raina. She always supported his creativity. And even thought he doesn't know why but since the Valentines dance he's felt like he made a mistake. And Raina does too. Raina and Sheena are walking together through the hallway.

"So, how long are you gonna continue to avoid him?" Sheena asks.

"I'm not avoiding him. I'm just not gonna put myself in that position anymore," Raina says to her.

"What position is that?"

"You know what, I'm not gonna be throwing myself at him."

"Raina you never threw yourself at him to begin with. You two are just drawn to each other," Sheena says to her.

"Well not anymore."

"Okay, if you say so. I'm so over both of you anyway." Sheena says frustrated.

"What's that supposed to mean?"

"It's like everybody and their mama can see that you two should be together but you. I know you feel like he has Lissa and you don't wanna be that other chick but sometimes you gotta take what you want in life. Or just be miserable alone."

"The way I see it Sheen its Dan that has to make up his mind. I'm not gonna put myself out there if he's gonna stay with her."

Down the hall near the main office Dan is looking at some leaflets form different colleges. He looks up and sees Raina and Sheena walking his way.

"Hey y'all" Dan says to them.

"What's up?" Sheena says to him. Raina doesn't say anything.

"Looking at colleges," Sheena says to him to break the uncomfortable silence between them.

"Yeah, just checking them all out. I'm thinking about going for journalism." Raina looks at him a little surprised.

"I hope you make the right choice," Sheena says to him.

"I think I know what I want now." Dan replies.

Raina looks at him then looks away. "I gotta get to class."

"Raina … I got a new poetry book I think you might like."

"I … can't read that now, I'm in the middle of reading another book. See ya," Raina walks away down the hall.

"So how long is she gonna hate me?" Dan asks Sheena.

"She doesn't hate you. But you do make it hard for her to like you."

"How? What did I do?"

"Dan why are you still messing around with Lissa's funky ass when you're in love with Raina?" Sheena asks him.

"In love? I like her but ..."

"But what? Lissa giving it up so good that you can't let her go?"

"That's not fair Sheena."

"The truth isn't always pretty. What else do you need to happen before you wake up and see it?"

"It's not that easy Sheena."

"Yes Dan ... it is. See ya later."

After school, Dan is by his car waiting for Lissa and he starts reading the brochures and Lissa walks up to him.

"Hey, baby."

"Hey." She gives him a kiss.

"Listen, I got some brochures from all the colleges with the best law programs. I was thinking we could go over them and pick out the best one for us."

"Ah, yeah I was thinking ..."

Lissa sees the other brochures in his hand.

"What are those?"

"Yeah, I was looking at some other schools for journalism."

"Why, I thought we decided that we were going to go to law school together?"

"I was just thinking I should keep my options open."

"When did you decide this?" Lissa asks him upset.

"Actually, I've been thinking about this for awhile now. You know how much I like writing and Raina saw some of my work and she likes ..."

Lissa hears her name and snaps.

"What's that bitch got to do with this?!"

"Don't call her that, she's not a bitch."

"So this is about that *bitch*?" Lissa yells pissed off.

"Hey chill out, I feel like I should do this."

"So your listening to her now?! We already decided what we're going to do!"

"No, you decided what we were going to do not me. I was just dumb not to say anything."

"So now it's dumb? We're in a relationship Dan you're supposed to talk to me about decisions like that. Me, your girlfriend, not some lame ass bitch!"

Dan exhales deeply and is tired of her calling Raina a bitch.

"No, this is about you trying to control every thing we do in this relationship! I'm sick of this shit!"

"We both know those stupid little stories aren't going to provide a future for us!"

"Stupid? You know what this conversation is over." Dan says through clench teeth.

"What do you mean over? We're going to resolve this shit now!"

Dan looks at her and thinks to himself enough is enough. He's been wondering if he should do this or not but her attitude has just made this decision a whole lot easier.

"Correction, we're over!"

"What do you mean over?" Lissa asks to him stunned.

"We're done?"

"Just like that? After everything I've given you?"

Dan turns glares at her then he opens his car door and starts his engine. Then he reverses out of the parking spot and drives away. Lissa is left standing there in disbelief about what just happened.

Chapter 10

<u>House Party- April 1st 1995</u>

It was Saturday night and it's the first night of spring break. Most college students are heading for Daytona Beach for Black Beach weekend or to Atlanta for the annual Freaknik. Even with all that going on outside of St. Petersburg there are a few college undergraduates that still come to Da Burg for the jump off also. Many go to the Clearwater beach or to Yabor City to the clubs. But tonight there's a house party in Da Burg that one of the frats is throwing.

Marcus and Sheena are waiting in Raina's living room downstairs while she gets ready to go. Tonight she decided to stop pining over Dan and see who else she could meet in this town. Its times like this she would really miss Cleveland and her old friends Joy and LeTasha but Marcus and Sheena treat her just like family. Granted that Marcus is the older annoying brother she never had.

"Hey girl, what you doing in there?!" Sheena yells to her upstairs.

"Hold on, I'm coming," Raina yells from the bathroom.

"Give her time; she gotta put her face on straight," Marcus sarcastically cracks.

"Shut up Marcus!"

"Come on, I don't wanna be the last ones there," Sheena yells.

Raina walks downstairs dress in a sexy red midriff and hip hugging jeans.

"Okay, I'm ready."

"Where are your folks?" Marcus asks.

"They went to a doctor's seminar in Tallahassee they'll be back tomorrow. Whose party is this again?"

"Catriona said it's a frat party by some brothers at FAMU."

"It's gonna be off the hook and ah, your boy is going to be there too," Marcus mentions to Raina.

"My boy, what are you talking about?" Raina asks him.

"You know who I'm talking about, you know he broke up with old girl right?" Marcus says happily.

"What? When did that happen?"

"Yeah and how come I didn't know about it until now?" Sheena asks.

"Hey Dan just told me what happen yesterday."

"Did he say why they broke up?" Raina inquires.

Marcus shrugs, "He really didn't say why."

"I guess we better get there then," Sheena says excited.

They drive in Marcus's car to the house where the party is at and parked all down the block. There in the Harbor Dale neighborhood on 26th Avenue South. People are standing outside drinking in front of a huge two-story house. This was the hood for sure. They get out of the car and walk up to the house. They hear "First of the Month" by Bone Thugs & Harmony from outside and Raina is reminded of Cleveland. The smell of weed and alcohol fill the air.

"This is what I'm talking about," Sheena exclaims.

"Yeah, this is taking me back to Cleveland."

They walk inside and see people dancing and drinking. Some guy's are wearing frat sweaters and some girls have on Sigma Phi sorority colors. Dan is standing to the side with a drink in his hand. He spots Raina walking through with Sheena and Marcus to the middle where everybody is dancing. In the middle of the dance floor is a frat brother dancing all over a girl dressed in daisy dukes and a tank top. His hands are clasping on to her ass and his tongue's half way down her throat. Raina walks by, and he looks up at her.

Marcus and Sheena are dancing together and Raina starts to dance by herself. The DJ play's a reggae song by Chapelton, 'Tour' and Raina is dancing to the beat and gaining the attention of guys around her. Lissa is also at the party and sees Raina and glares at her. Cory walks up to Lissa and sees her looking at Raina.

"Hey what's up?" he asks her.

"Nothing, what do you want?" Lissa says coldly.

"Damn girl, I was just going to offer you a drink that's all."

"Oh, okay."

"Do you want another glass of hater-aide 'cuz you look like you're kinda low?"

Lissa flicks him off and cuts her eyes at him as Cory smiles and walks away. The frat brother who was all over the other girl walks up behind Raina and starts to grind on her. Raina keeps on dancing and as if it was, a dance move turns and faces him. The brother moves back behind her again and Raina moves again. They repeat this again and Dan walks up to Raina and she turns around and grinds on him erotically, the frat brother then walks away.

"You look like you could use a hand." Dan says.

"Thanks."

They continue to dance together and Lissa watches them with resentment. The DJ mixes into a slow song by R&B group Subway called 'Fire'.

The same feeling that Raina has been trying so hard to deny come back again. Sheena and Marcus see them dancing together and smile. "Hey … lets go outside for a minute." Dan says to Raina.

"Okay."

As they walk out the front door Lissa steps in front of Dan, "So this is who you're leaving me for? This bitch!"

"Aye yo, who you calling a *bitch*?!" Raina says and gets up in her face and Dan holds her back and trying to keep some "U. N. I. T. Y" in the place.

Dan looks at Lissa, "What part of we're over don't you understand girl?"

"We're not done until I say we are!"

"Aight, you keep on believing that if you want to," Dan takes Raina by the hand and walks by Lissa and goes outside.

"I'm sorry about that." Dan apologizes.

"It's not your fault. That girl is just crazy."

"Marcus just told me you two broke up. What happen?"

"What didn't happen," Dan jokes, "I think I knew we were growing apart, I just didn't wanna admit to myself."

"I know what you mean."

"When we were playing Truth or Dare and you said what you thought being in love was, what made you say that?"

"I don't know, I … just said what I felt," Raina says to him as they reach his car.

"Well I guess I should have said this to you a long time ago."

"What is it?" Raina asks.

Dan looks her in the eyes. "I'm in love with you."

Raina eyebrows raised, "Dan I don't think we should rush into anything."

"I think we've been holding back for too long as it is." Dan stares her in her eyes and Raina tries to think of a reason not to give in to her feelings.

"Listen, I'm not trying to be a rebound thing …"

"Trust me, you're not," Dan leans into her and gives her a kiss. Surprised by his kiss she hesitates but then slowly opens her mouth, touching his tongue with hers.

Dan drives Raina back to her house and holds her hand as he drives. The entire drive they don't say anything to each other. When they arrive at her house, Dan parks his car in the driveway and he walks to her front door. Raina opens the door. She turns around and smiles at him faintly and so does he. They embrace each other gently and Dan looks down into her eyes and he caress her face Raina softly kisses her lips against his.

Raina not wanting to lose herself in the moment pulls away and so does Dan. An awkward silence falls over them and Raina steps inside the house then turns and looks at him.

"Come on," She says to him.

"Where's your folks at?"

"Out of town."

Raina takes him by the hand and walks him upstairs to her bedroom. Raina closes the door behind her and turns and faces Dan. He takes his fingers and runs it down her face and neck until he reaches her breast. She reaches up and unbuttons his shirt and pulls it off of him. Dan then pulls her midriff over her head and they both stare at each other topless. Dan kisses her lips then he steps back, unzips her pants, pulls them down. He smiles when he sees her thickness in black lace panties. Dan takes a condom out of his wallet and pulls down his boxers and puts it on. Raina eyes light up when she sees the size of his penis is. She lies on her bed in just her black lace panties and Dan steps to the bed and pulls them off of her. He climbs on top of her and kisses her lips and neck and then looks her in the eyes. He takes her hard nipples between his lips, and alternates kissing, sucking and tugging on them. Raina feels herself becoming wetter. Dan looks up and Raina smiles as if given him permission to go further. Dan reaches down and positions his penis at the opening of her vagina and rubs her moistness against his tip and her clitoris and then gently pushes inside of her. Raina flinches from his size and her mouth opens and she exhales.

"Are you okay?" Dan asks.

"Yeah ... I'm good," Raina smiles. Soon her vagina conforms to his size as Dan strokes her slowly. His hardness fills her tight canal. They gaze into each other's eyes lovingly as he penetrates deeper into her with every new stroke. Raina closes her eyes and enjoys it as Dan spreads her legs further apart and increases his speed. Her nails dig into his back. His lips suck on her neck. They trade positions with Raina moving on top of Dan and she begins to ride him. She whines her hips like did at the party to the reggae rhythm. Dan stares at her beautiful naked body dancing on top of him and caresses from her breast to her thighs. Both Raina and Dan are so lost in this moment that they can't believe this is finally happening after all these months. The hours feel like minutes while there together.

Dan slides out of Raina then moves behind her and re-enters her warm walls from the back. Raina arches her back and works her hips back toward him. Dan grabs her waistline and begins to control the deepest of each stroke into her wetness, alternating speeds. Raina clenches on to her pillow as Dan moves in and out of her. An overwhelming sensation flutters from her stomach and travels down to her vagina and Raina gasps as her orgasm comes over her and her wetness flows out. She falls forward pulling Dan's penis out and turns on her back and looks at him. She stares at his fully erect manhood with her juices still on it and smiles.

"You feel so good," Dan says to her as he continues to bring her pleasure. Raina opens her eyes touches his face and he slows down, smiles at her affectionately and kisses her. And for the first time in his life Dan makes love to a woman.

Chapter 11

Girl Fight- April 2nd 1995

Raina wakes up in bed naked under her sheets feeling exhausted but good. She laughs to her herself about what finally happened last night with Dan. He didn't leave until early in the morning. Her phone rings and Raina looks at her alarm clock and sees that it's 10:35 AM and picks up her phone and sees' that the caller I.D. says **SHEENA CAMPBELL 727-822-1639**. Raina smiles and answers the phone.

"Hello?"

"You better tell me every little detail of what happen last night!" Sheena demands. Raina starts to laugh out loud.

"I wanna know what happen from the time you left to this very second girl! I want it blow by blow!" Sheena yells.

"Dang ... can a girl live?"

"Don't make me come over there! You know I will!"

"Well ... we talked for a minute outside of the party. Then he drove me home. Then he left," Raina nonchalantly says to her.

"That's it? That's all that happened?" Sheena asks her bewildered.

"Yeah he left about 3:30 in the morning." Raina says to her.

"3:30 in the morning ...What?!"

Raina starts to laugh again.

"You two did the nasty!"

"Front, back and side to side," Raina says and smiles.

"Oh my god! How did it happen?"

"Sheena, when we got here we just started kissing and I

took him to my bedroom. Then it was like we just knew we were going to do it. So we just started undressing each other and it jumped off."

"What ... was it good?" Sheena inquires timidly.

"I'll just say this, Dan knows what he's doing."

Sheena starts to laugh, "Did it hurt?"

Sheena asks wanting to know what to prepare for.

"Yeah but in a very good way. Let's just say Dan cleaned all my cobwebs out."

"Wow ... I see why Lissa was so sprung. I saw what she did last night before y'all left."

"Yeah, that bitch was lucky Dan was holding me back. I was gonna whip that bitch's ass."

"God I wish I was over there when she did that so I coulda stomped her face in with you!" Sheena exclaims, "Did you fight a lot up in Cleveland?"

"Sheen, I'm light-skinned and I got straight hair. So you know when I was younger I had to fight a bitch picking on me every other day! They used just walk up to me and pop me in the back of the head for nothing! I had to fight back. It was a matter of survival. When I got older they left me alone."

"Damn! So you're like Mike Tyson without the speech impediment!" Sheena quips and Raina laughs.

"Girl you're stupid!" Raina exclaims.

"So what's gonna happen now between you and Dan?"

"I don't know ... we didn't exactly do that much talking last night."

"Yeah just a whole lot of grunting!"

"Shut up," Raina laughs.

"So what time are your folks coming back?"

"This afternoon."

"Do you wanna hook up and go to the mall?"

"Yeah that's cool."

"Do you want me to call Marcus and tell him to meet us there with Dan?" Sheena requests.

"Yeah ... do that." Raina says to her.

♥♥♥

A few hours later at Tyrone Square Mall, Raina and Sheena are sitting in the food court eating from Chick-Fil-A. On the outside, Dan and Marcus are driving in the parking lot looking for an empty spot. Dan turns down another isle looking for a spot.

"So you finally woke the hell up and got with Raina? About got-damn time!" Marcus declares.

"Yeah ... it was." Dan says to him.

"So how was it compared to Lissa?" Marcus asks.

"Well, it's kinda like comparing apples and orange's. Lissa is freak. It's like she likes to be so in control all the time. It's not that it's wack - far from that. But sometimes you want a girl to be a little submissive and just let it happen. But with Raina it was more ... intense. It was just so natural."

"I bet, you two have been playing this cat and mouse game for about nine months now. Both of y'all wore probably so backed up I'm surprised y'all ain't explode," Marcus says to him.

They get out of Dan's Ford Probe SE and he beeps on the alarm.

Marcus looks at him, "So are you and Raina now officially dating?"

"Not really we really did talk about that. I guess we'll see what's up now."

They walk into the mall and see Sheena and Raina at a table eating and walk over to them.

"Hey baby." Marcus says to Sheena and kisses her and sits down next to her. "Hey," Dan says to Raina.

"Hey." She smiles and he sits next to her. They both stare at each other and grin uncontrollably. Sheena and Marcus look at them and smile too.

"So how you uh, how you doing Raina? Huh? Gotta a big, uh, big smile over there? Gotta, gotta nice little story you wanna tell us? You and Dan had been playing this game for nine months? Huh? Gotta, gotta little backed up there? Yeah? Gotta a lot of sexual frustration to release? Huh? Gotta a little hot down there? Building up, building up that energy for quite some time? Huh?" Marcus continues as *his voice is getting higher in pitch.* "Yeah, no sex for a long time now? Finally got a chance to let it loose? Did a few positions? From the back, front, side to side? Some fantasies got fulfilled, some new fantasies were made? At the end of the night you're both you are exhausted by experience? Yeah? Yeah?" Marcus brings his voice down a notch. "So, so, what did you do last night?" Marcus rants off hysterically.

Raina stares at Marcus trying to hold a straight face, while Sheena and Dan are laughing their asses off.

"Shut the hell up Marcus! I swear I'm gonna kick your ass!" Raina yells at him.

Everybody is laughing now.

"Come on you fool! Let's give them some time alone." Sheena says to Marcus as they get up and leave.

"We'll be back." Sheena says to Raina.

"Aight." Raina looks at Dan.

"I swear I hate his ass." Raina says laughing.

"That nigga is a fool," Dan says and then they look into each other's eyes. They both lean forward and French kiss each other passionately.

"Did you make it in okay?" Raina asks him.

"Yeah, my folks didn't even hear me come in. So are you alright?"

"Yeah, I'm good."

"So I guess we really didn't talk last night." Dan says to her.

"I guess not."

"So I guess I should ask. Do you wanna ... kick it with me?"

"I don't know let me think about. I'll get back to you about it," Raina says sarcastically.

"I swear I'll kill you girl if you leave me hanging," Dan

says laughing.

Raina leans forward kiss him again.

A week later, everybody is back in school trying to get over the hump till graduation. For the first time ever Dan drove Raina to school and they instantly caught the eye of everybody walking together through the hallway. Lissa sat with her friend Tamara at a table fuming at the sight of them together.

"I know she stole him from me. I'm gonna deal with that bitch soon enough." Lissa says to her.

Raina and Dan however are not aware of the hate that they've caused. "I can't believe I'm walking here with you like this," Dan says to Raina.

"Me either, I didn't think you would ever leave Lissa."

"Something I should have done a long time ago. My mom nearly did a back flip when I told her I dumped Lissa and I'm with you."

"You told your mom? Dang now I'm gonna feel weird going over there now." Raina says to him.

"Don't worry about that, my mom loves you. She couldn't stand Lissa."

"Well that's good to know!" Raina exclaims.

Cory is walking down the hallway and sees Raina and Dan together holding hands and shakes his head.

"What's up love birds?"

"What's up Cory?" Dan asks him.

Raina rolls her eyes and looks at Dan.

"Hey, I gotta get to my Bio class. I'll see you after fourth period right," Raina says to Dan.

"Yeah okay," Raina kisses Dan and walks down the hallway to her class.

"She hates me don't she?" Cory asks Dan.

"Ah … yeah pretty much. Yeah, she's not that fond of you."

"I seem to have that affected on women. So you pulled her in. I knew you two were gonna end up hooking up together."

"You did?"

"Yeah man it was obvious."

"And you're okay with that," Dan asks him.

"Of course dawg, I'm a pimp! Besides ain't no girl gonna fade our friendship."

Dan laughs and gives him some dap.

"Cory, you're my dawg."

They start to walk to class.

"So did you hit it already," Cory asks him.

Dan shakes his head, "Mind your business nigga."

"Come on man. You gotta tell me," Cory pleads him.

"No, I don't gotta tell ya."

"Ah … what I'm I thinking you ain't hit that ass yet! Did you?"

"Stop trippin'."

"Come on man I thought we were dawgs! Okay, okay, blink twice if you touched it." Cory continues to harass Dan until they get to class.

After school Raina is walking out of the building to the parking lot to find Dan. Lissa walks up behind her and shoves her in the back. Raina stumbles forward but is able to regain her balance.

"I told you to stay away from my man bitch!"

Under normal circumstances Lissa would never try Raina like this but with the right motivation by Tamara anybody could be motivated to act out of character. Unfortunately for Lissa despite her angrier she's never really been in a fight since second grade.

"That's it!" Raina yells and walks up to Lissa and punches her in the mouth splitting her bottom lip. Lissa staggers back in shock by the blow.

"Oh my god, I'm bleeding!"

"I been told you that you had one more time to try me before I whip your ass!"

"Bitch!"

Lissa filled of rage charges back at Raina like a linebacker. Only problem being is Lissa was only 5"2 and 112 pounds. Raina was 5"5 and 125 pounds so Raina easily shoved Lissa off. Going into a rage Lissa does what most girls try and do in a fight and pulls Raina's hair. Unfortunately for Lissa again, Raina loses her balance and falls on top of her. Raina begins to punch her in the face with her fist. After months of holding back she's finally able to unleash on her. Lissa covers her face and quickly regrets trying her but refuses to give up. Soon a small crowd sees them fighting and rushes around them.

"Girl fight!" one guy yells. Unaware of the situation Dan, Marcus and Sheena are walking toward the commotion. Suddenly Dan gets a bad vibe when he hears what the guy yelled.

"Girl fight? You don't think it's …"

"Oh shit," Sheena yells and sees Raina on top of Lissa pounding Lissa in the head. Dan, Sheena and Marcus rush over to them and Dan and Sheena pull Raina off of Lissa. Marcus holds back Lissa.

"Let me go," Lissa screams.

"Go ahead let her go so I can whoop her ass some more," Raina yells.

"Dan, get her out of here before a teacher comes out here," Marcus yells.

Sheena and Dan take Raina to his car. "Are you okay girl?"

"Yeah that bitch just pulled my hair."

"What happened?" Dan asks her.

"That little bitch pushed me in the back so I busted her lip!"

"Damn, why couldn't she do that when I was there so we could both beat her ass?!" Sheena yells.

"You're both crazy! You both could get suspended before graduation," Dan says to them.

"I don't care. If she tries me again I'll stomp her head in!"

Marcus runs to the car.

"Aye, let's get out of here," Marcus yells.

"Where's Lissa?"

"She dipped when a teacher came around the corner and so did I," Marcus replies.

"Come on lets go!" Dan yells and they all get in the car and pull off.

Chapter 12

"Prom" - April 27ᵗʰ 1995

Raina and Lissa have not bump heads with each other since the fight outside of school a couple of weeks ago. After the anger subsided and the bruise came out Lissa was a bit hesitant to fight with Raina again. Instead all they do is exchange dirty looks to each other as they pass in the hallways. Relationship wise, Dan and Raina were still in romantic bliss with each other. Although they have only made love once, they were both dying to be alone with each other again. Prom night was finally here and tonight was their night. Her mother was helping Raina get dress in her prom dress. Raina has on a blue one shoulder long dress with a pleated a-line skirt.

"You look beautiful," her mom affirms.

"Thanks Mom."

"Let me fix your hair."

"So Dad's working late again?"

Her mother is quite for a second, "Yeah, another double at the hospital."

"Are you okay?"

"Yes, come on let's get you're shoes on."

Raina slips on her shoes.

"There you go, you're simply beautiful."

They hug each other. They hear the doorbell ring.

"I'll get it."

Her mother opens the door and it's Dan, Sheena, Marcus, and Cory and his date.

"Hey guys."

"Hey Mrs. Williams," Dan says. He gives her a hug.

"She'll be out in second. Ray, their here."

Raina comes down the stairs.

"Hey y'all," Raina says to them.

"Damn, you look good," Dan says to her and she smiles.

"You look half way civilized," Marcus says and Sheena elbows him. Raina flicks him off.

"I think we should go but first this is for you," Dan gives her a corsage.

"It's beautiful, thank you."

"You two are too cute. You guys have fun tonight," her mother says to them.

"See ya later Mom."

Everyone in the gym was dressed to impress as they dance to Biggie's, 'One More Chance - Remix.' They all go and take prom pictures together; Cory's date is with them. Raina and Dan pose together in front of the St. Petersburg Pier backdrop.

"That dress is so sexy on you," Dan says as he kisses her neck.

"Just wait until you see it off me."

"Can't wait."

As the photographer takes their picture together, the DJ puts on Aaliyah's 'At Your Best – Remix' and Sheena and Marcus begins to dance. Raina and Dan do also. Cory's dancing with a girl and Lissa dancing with another guy and sees them. Dan and Raina are completely into each other.

"I love you."

Raina looks in his eyes, "I love you too."

"You know that's the first time you've said that to me."

"I know, I've been scared to say it."

"Don't be," Dan says and kisses her lips.

"I need a drink."

"I got ya."

Dan goes to get some punch. The table is on the other side of the gym. Lissa walks up to him. She caresses his back and Dan smiles thinking it was Raina and turns and sees Lissa wearing a black satin strapless cocktail dress. Her hair was parted in the middle the ends in curls. She smiled seductively looking like the sexy vixen she was.

"Hey Daniel. Enjoying yourself?"

Dan glares at her for a second then fixes a glass of punch for Raina.

"I was… what do you want?"

"Why you gotta be like that?"

"You know why. That shit you pulled with Raina was stupid."

"She had it coming," Lissa says angrily.

"Whatever, I gotta go." Dan starts to walk away.

"Dan, I'm late," Lissa says and Dan turns and looks at her. "I'm late Daniel."

He shakes his head, "You know I didn't think you would be so desperate to break us up but I guess I was wrong."

"I don't expect anything from you, I just wanted to let you know."

"I don't believe you."

"Hmm … You remember the last time we had sex? Remember how good it felt when I let you hit raw," Dan has an uneasy expression on his face. "I thought you would." Lissa turns and walks away. Dan regrettably remembers that he did have sex with her a few times without a condom. Raina walks up to him.

"What's taking you so long?"

"Nothing, I just ran into somebody I knew. I got a little caught up."

♥♥♥

That Monday at school Dan walks through the hallway quickly looking for Lissa. All weekend he was thinking about what she said to him at prom. He sees her standing with her friends outside and walks up to her.

"We need to talk."

"About what Daniel?"

"You know what," Dan grabs her by her arm and pulls her away from her friends.

"What kind of shit are you trying to pull?"

"I'm not pulling anything," Lissa says to him seriously.

"So are you pregnant?"

"Yes I am. What do you care?"

"Don't play with me, if that's my baby I do care."

"*If?* You were the only guy I've ever been with. Don't stress yourself I'm having an abortion."

"Don't kill my baby Lissa. Please?"

"So you're gonna be there Dan, you gonna help me raise it? I got my whole life ahead of me, I don't need a baby!"

"Listen to me, if you're pregnant I'll take care of my responsibilities, alright?"

Lissa looks into his eyes, "Dan … I just don't wanna do this alone."

"You won't … have you told you're mom?"

"No not yet."

Raina comes in from school and sees her parents in the living room. Both of them are sitting on the couch waiting for her. Raina knows that's never a good sign.

"Hey… what's up?"

"Hey baby girl, we need to talk to you for a minute," her dad says.

Her mom gestures toward the sofa, "Have a seat honey."

"What's going on?"

"Honey, there's something we need to tell you that might be a little hard to say," Martin says to her.

"Okay"

"Your father and I have talked about this and we have decided to separate for a while."

"What?"

"Honey, we have been going through a very difficult time and we think it's best if we take some time away from each other to figure things out," Martin explains.

"Figure things out, so you're getting a divorce?"

"No, we just need some time to decide if we should stay together," her mother clarifies.

Raina still can't believe what is happening, "What about counseling or something?"

"We been going for a while now, Ray I'm going back to Cleveland after you graduate, you can stay here with your father or come with me if you want to."

Raina shakes her head, "You know ... I know you guys are not perfect but how the hell did this happen? I thought moving here and starting over is something you too wanted?"

"Something your father wanted," Her mother utters.

Her father glares at her, "Don't blame me for this."

"Then who should I blame Martin? You're the one who took this job down here without even discussing it with me. I had to give up a career in Cleveland that I worked ten years to establish. You always think of yourself first before your family."

"Everything I've done is for us. This job was a chance of a lifetime," Martin says to her.

"A chance of a lifetime for you Martin not us."

And for the first time Raina sees them being honest with each other, "So we gave up everything for what? How could you do this to us? How can you be so selfish Dad?"

"Honey, there's a lot more involved than you realize."

"Whatever. I'm out," Raina has a look of disbelief on her face and gets up and walks out the front door.

As Raina is walking down the street trying to digest what just happened, Dan pulls up next to her in his Probe. She gets in and he parks his car. Dan looks very upset and Raina notices it.

"Hey, what's bothering you?"

"Lissa ... told me something at prom."

"What is it?"

Dan tries to find the words to say for a moment, "She told me that she was … late."

Raina leans back and has a look of disappointment on her face.

"At first I didn't believe her but I just talked to her and I think she being real with me."

"What are you going to do?"

"She wanted to get an abortion but I told her I will take care of it, if it's my baby," Dan lets this soak in then continues, "This is not going to come between us."

"Dan, she's having your baby, how can that not affect us?"

"I love you and I'm going to be with you. Nothing is going to change that."

"You're going to be tied to her for the rest of your life and I don't need that stress. I got enough to deal with already."

"What are you saying?"

"You have your own problems and so do I."

"What problems?" Dan asks her confused.

"Dan, I'm moving back to Cleveland after graduation. I'm going to go to school up there."

"What? You're just all of a sudden picking up and leaving? That doesn't make any sense! Why?"

"You got your own responsibilities to take care of now."

"You're important to me too! I'm not choosing her over you!"

"Dan, just do what you have to do."

"But what about us?"

"I need some space Dan … I need a break," Raina gets out of the car and walks away tears fill her eyes. Dan gets out of the car and looks baffled by her reaction.

"Raina wait!"

She ignores him and continues to walk away as tears roll down her face. Dan feels that everything is happening is his fault.

Raina decided to go to Sheena's house down the street instead of going home and seeing her parents. In the past few months Sheena and her has formed a friendship closer then any of her friends back in Cleveland. Raina is in Sheena's room stressing out about what's happening to her.

"I can't believe all this shit," Raina says as she sits on Sheena's bed.

"I'm so sorry this is happening to you."

"You didn't make this happen Sheena, my dad is why I'm going through this."

"I know that this isn't easy for you but if you never came down here, I wouldn't have found my best friend. I know that sounds selfish."

"No you don't, before I met you I didn't have too many friends I could count on, ya know? It's like I was just there for their convenience but you you're my girl," Raina gives Sheena a hug.

"I should be hugging you," Sheena says and laughs. "So as your friend I can be honest with you and tell you that I think pushing Dan away now is a mistake."

"He's got to many issues right now and I got my own shit to deal with."

"I just don't trust Lissa's ass!"

"It's not just her, it's like all the men in my life find a way to hurt me, besides my mom needs me now."

"I still think you're making a mistake but I understand where ya coming from. I'm gonna miss you girl."

♥♥♥

Dan decided to go tell Marcus what happen and met him at Bartlett Park. Marcus is playing basketball with Cory and some other guys. Dan walks over to the court and Marcus goes over to him.

"What's up Dan?"

"Raina broke up with me."

"Why?"

"Lissa told me at prom that she was late."

"Oh man, I swear the girl is like herpes she just won't go away," Marcus yells.

"Yeah well I told Raina and she flipped out on me."

"Just give her some time she'll get over it."

"I don't got time. She said she's moving back to Cleveland after graduation."

"Damn, when did that happen?"

"As soon as I told her about Lissa she dropped this on me."

"So what you gonna do?"

"There's nothing I can do. I just gotta take care of this shit," Dan says frustrated.

"Hey, if this was any other girl I'd tell you to bump her and move on but I've never seen you so in sync with another chick. Yo, you gotta man up and get your woman. I don't wanna see you sulking around here crying like Babyface around me. And I damn sure don't wanna see you with Lissa ass," Marcus begs.

"You stupid dawg," Dan says and laughs. "I'm holla at ya later." Dan gives him some dap and leaves.

Two weeks later the senior class is in the gym for a dress rehearsal for graduation. Everybody's dressed in his or her cap and gown and Raina and Sheena are standing to the side. Dan is talking to Lissa and Raina sees them. Dan looks up and sees Raina and walks over to her.

"Hey."

"Hey Dan," Sheena replies but Raina doesn't say anything and there's an awkward silence. "I'm gonna give you guys some space." Sheena walks away.

"Raina, can we please talk?"

"I don't have anything to say."

"Well I do, I don't wanna lose you like this, I need you."

She rolls her eyes, "Lissa and your baby need you more."

"Why are you pushing me away? What's going on?"

"Lissa's having a baby, remember," she walks away. Sheena walks up to Dan.

"Why is she acting like that Sheena?"

"Dan, before you told her about Lissa, her parents told her that they were separating. She may act like she doesn't want you but she does."

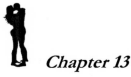

Chapter 13

"If This Isn't Love" - May 19th 1995

A week later Dan is in Lissa's house in the same room where he's had plenty of sex with her in. In hindsight he now wishes he would've kept it in his pants. Lissa dressed in a pair of short shorts and a pink tank top and was hoping Dan's member wanted to come out and play.

"I can't believe it's all over. It's like we've been waiting for this day for so long and now that it's here it doesn't feel real," Lissa says to him. Dan seems to be oblivious to what she is saying and lost in thought.

"Hey, earth to Daniel, where are you?"

"Sorry I just got something on my mind."

"You mean Raina ... I heard about you two. I know you might not believe me but I am sorry to see you going through this," Dan stares at Lissa round ass in her shorts. Lissa smiles at him. "You deserve better."

She walks over and gives him a hug and Dan hugs her back. Then Lissa softly kisses his neck and then gives him little baby kisses until she reaches his lips. Then she gives him a soft passionate kiss and Dan kisses her back. His hands caress her ass. Lissa gets wet from his touch. Dan pulls away and smiles at her.

"You don't know how much I've missed the way you use to touch me," Lissa says to Dan as he holds her in his arms.

"Me too. I guess us having this baby was just meant to be."

"*We* were meant to be together. Nobody is gonna love you like I do," Lissa says and feels on his hard on in his pants.

"True ... but I'm thinking that since were about to be this instant family we should make sure."

"What do you mean?" Lissa asks confuse.

Dan reaches in his backpack and pulls out an EPT box. Lissa frowns, "What's that for?"

"What do you think? It's been a couple of weeks now and you still look the same to me," Dan says bluntly.

"Daniel ... you still don't believe me?"

"Well, just piss on this stick and take all my doubt away," Dan says as he hands her the box.

Lissa steps back, "I don't have to pee right now."

"Go drink some water. We got time."

"I don't know why you're making such a big deal out of this," Lissa says and goes and sits on her bed.

"I should've known. How long was you gonna keep this lie going? What was you gonna do? Fake a miscarriage a month from now," Dan asks her angrily. An anxious expression comes across her face.

"Daniel ... I can explain baby ..."

"Explain what, how you been lying to me!"

Lissa jumps up and grabs his arm, "Baby, listen to me, I know why you broke up with me I don't blame you. So I thought if we can start over again I could show you how much I love you."

Dan pulls his arm away and looks her up and down.

"You don't even know what love is," Dan says and walks out of her room.

Raina pulls up to the house in her father's car. She gets out, walks toward the door, and sees Dan waiting at her front door. She stops and Dan walks toward her. Tonya sees them through the window.

"What are you doing here?"

"I had something to tell you. Lissa was lying she never was pregnant." Raina is shock but doesn't say anything, "She was just trying to get me back. Sheena told me about your parents, why didn't you say anything?"

"I don't want to talk about them."

"Why not?"

"They have nothing to do with us."

"Bullshit. Why didn't you tell me?" Dan says and steps closer to her. Raina fights to hold back the tears in her eyes.

"Because there's nothing you can do about it!"

"Raina don't push me away, I can help you …"

"You can't help me Dan, you can't fix this! All you do is complicate shit for me," Raina yells, she can't hold the tears back anymore.

"I'm not you're dad Raina. I would never hurt you like that," Dan caress her face.

"You don't know what you're talking about," Raina tries to walk by him and Dan grabs her arm.

"Raina, don't runaway from me-" she pulls away.

"Leave me alone! Please?"

"I love you Raina."

Raina looks at him and she feels the same way too but turns away and walks inside of the house. Dan is left standing in her driveway with his heart broken.

Raina goes in her room and starts to pack her suitcase. Her mind was still on Dan. She wanted him to hold her but it was all too much to deal with. In her mind she knew she couldn't stay in St. Pete with her dad. Her mom walks to her doorway and watches her pack.

"Are you okay baby?"

"Yeah, I'm fine. I'm almost packed."

Her mother walks in and sits next to her suitcase, "You know, what's going on between your father and me doesn't need to affect your relationship with Dan."

"What relationship?"

"I saw him outside."

Raina doesn't say anything.

"Do you love him?"

"Mom ... every time I let somebody in they always find a way to hurt me."

"Honey, running away from your problems doesn't solve them. If what you have with Dan is real, then don't let it go."

"Do you still love dad?"

"Yes. I do," she gets up and walks out of her room. Raina sits down on her bed and looks at the picture of her dad and her together at Busch Gardens a few months ago. She gets up and walks to the den and sees her dad looking though a photo album. He looks up and sees Raina and they don't say anything. Then Raina walks in and sits next to him and leans her head on his shoulder.

Two days later at Tampa International Airlines the elevator doors open and Dan walks out. He goes to the monitor and sees Flight 870 to Cleveland, Gate A3. He makes his way to the shuttle and rides it to the terminal. He rushes to gate A3 and sees the doors close and the flight attendant about to leave. He walks over to the attendant.

"Excuse me but did you see a black girl about this tall, hair a little pass her shoulders?"

"Uh, yeah she boarded the plane a few minutes ago. Is there a problem sir?"

"No, no problem at all," Dan says in a defeated tone. He starts to walk away. He walks by the restrooms and out of the ladies room comes Raina. She sees him walking away.

"Dan?"

Dan turns around and is shock to see her, "I ... I thought you were on the plane."

"I dropped off my mom. How did you know where I was?"

"Sheena told me you were going to the airport today. Obviously she didn't tell me you *weren't* leaving."

"I guess she wanted you to come get me."

"Remind me to kill her for torturing me like that. Are you okay?"

"Yeah I'm fine. You were right about everything. I know I was wrong but I was so angry ..." Dan takes a step closer to her. "I don't blame you for being upset with me ... I'm ..."

He takes another step and is right in front of her.

"I'm sorry Dan," Tears start to fill her eyes. Dan without a word wipes her tears away then he cups her face with his hands kisses her on the head and then kiss her lips.

"I love you Raina and as long as you love me. That's all that matters," Dan says to her.

"I love you too Dan."

Marlon McCaulsky, originally from Brooklyn, New York, is the best-selling author of The Pink Palace. *His goal is tell entertaining stories and to become a full-time novelist. He lives in Atlanta, Georgia with his wife of nine years.*

Sweet Thing

By

Jarold Imes

Chapter 1

It was hot like fire when Kandi decided to go into the corner mart on 23rd and Cleveland Avenue. With her hair pressed down and her Rayban sunglasses on her face, she could have been a dead ringer for Aaliyah if she had been a few shades lighter. She had gotten the orange and green Karl Kani shirt with the orange extra long shorts after being inspired by seeing Aaliyah and R. Kelly pull off a similar look in an outside photo shoot for *Right On!* magazine poster that she had taped to her wall. Kandi had resorted to tearing out pictures of Aaliyah, Da Brat, Xscape, TLC & SWV to show her moms the looks she was going for when she picked out her clothes and when she was trying to sing at local talent contests. Aside from giving herself five finger discounts, she always had a knack for singing and would always belt out a few notes when she could, especially when her man, Cortez and his boys, Kobe and Manuel were freestyling in a cipher at school. For the most part, her moms got the message. However when Ms. Priss, that's what Kandi called her mom behind her back wanted her to dress like a "lady" then she showed her pictures of Monica wearing styles she thought she could handle without giving up being a tom boy. Her mom never got into the "hood chick" look but she let her daughter wear what she wanted as long as it wasn't too masculine or "slutty" just to keep the peace in the house. With Kandi, unlike her older sister Vickie, she didn't have to worry about her acting slutty.

Kandi had one objective when she walked into the Garden Park Mart, not to make the same mistake her older sister Vickie did. Two years ago, Vickie was at one of the department stores when she attempted to try to boost some new high end fashions that she was going to resell out of the trunk of her boyfriend's beat up Toyota Camary. She had her customer's orders memorized and they gave her a sizable deposit to handle her business so she could get hers for the taking. Normally, Vickie took a few orders at a time so she could decrease her chances of getting caught. Vickie was the same height Kandi is now, but she was also about fifty pounds heavier. Being the quiet and polite big girl, at a first glance, no one would suspect her of taking anything. But this girl had been hitting up Belk, JCPenny, Dillards and Sears at the Hanes Mall and the Four Seasons Mall in Greensboro for three years. Last year, she added some malls in Charlotte, Durham, High Point and Salisbury to her repertoire and actually did a trial run in Richmond, Virginia and she was the reason the departments stores ate one hundred and fifty thousand dollars in losses. She herself brought home sixty g's, which was more than many married couples brought home to their household or one of the major drug boys did in the Tre-4, which was the prison inspired nickname for Winston Salem.

Kandi knew about Vickie's boosting schemed but she didn't know that she and two other females were in on some mail fraud schemes. One of the girls got caught and in an effort to reduce her sentence, not only did she drop the dime and Vickie and their co-defendant, she also told them about how Vickie managed to get the department stores for all their merchandise. So the girl sends Vickie for an order at JCPenny and Vickie gets arrested as she is walking out of the store to her car. In court, the girl sang another sad love song but made sure she hooked Vickie and their accomplice and before her sister could even breathe again, the judge had sentenced her to a seven to ten.

So when Kandi decided to try her hand at the trade her sister taught her four years ago when she was baby sitting for her mother who had to work a second shift, she followed a few simple rules. Number one, only boost what she needed. Mainly it was candy, feminine products, some mint flavored gum so she could have some when she had her alone time with Cortez and some other small stuff. Number two, she'd only hit low end stores that were owned by foreigners. Kandi had heard her parents cry all the time about how these Mexicans and Koreans and Arabs were coming to America, taking all their jobs and not even paying taxes on the money they was making. And then sending all the money back home and not investing in the country they were living in. She believed what she heard because she hardly ever saw black people own or work any of the small shops in her hood, even though she thought that black people made up the majority of the Tre-4. When she saw it that way, she felt justified cause all she was doing was making them pay taxes. If her parents had to pay taxes, then she felt that their foreign asses could pay taxes too. Instead of paying Uncle Sam, they were paying Kandi Bigelow. And lastly, she never told a soul. That was Vickie's biggest down fall and the reason why she and Kandi were writing letters back and forth in different detention centers they put her in all over the state of North Carolina. Kandi used to get mad cause it seemed like every time she wrote Vickie, that chick had a new address and then she had to remember what she put in the last letter that probably never reached her and retell those stories in addition to the new stuff she wanted to tell her. But aside form all that, Kandi's left hand never knew what her right hand was doing and sometimes she'd amaze herself because she pulled some things out of her right pocket that she didn't even know she'd put there.

Today, her shopping list consisted of her usual items but she really needed to make the trip so she could get some condoms. She specifically was looking for the ones that had a black and gold wrapper because she had seen what Cortez' member looked like when it was limp and she could only imagine what it look like when it was all grown up. She was scared too because she had heard one of the girls in the cafeteria talking about how big her man was and she saw that the space between her two hands was big enough to fit one of her size eight shoes through and still have some room. So them regular condoms wouldn't do. Even though she hadn't given it up yet, she was going to make him wear one because there were already questions about his paternity of two babies on at two different high schools in neighboring Kernersville. Naturally, Cortez denied them both though she suspected that he had in fact cheated on her and that one or possibly both of those babies were his. She didn't want to risk another chick boosting her man so she'd figure she'd handle that and be the grown woman she knew she was destined to be.

She had never boosted rubbers before and was concerned about the security tags that she saw on the boxes at Wal-Mart. She started to just open the boxes and just take them out and stuff a few of them in her pockets but she remembered the last person who did that ended up with their face on the floor with their hands behind their backs by time she got out of the store with her bag of Twizzler's and an Arabesque romance novel for her mama's birthday present secured safely in her pocket.

She figured her best shot would be to hit up a spot that she knew didn't have security cameras or any thing like that. A place where she could get in and out of and hide quickly. She even brought some money to pay for some of the things she wasn't going to steal so that she wouldn't look suspicious. After figuring out a way to get the condoms out of the boxes without being so obvious, she figured she'd be in and out and that it would be easy like a piece of cake. After all, who would suspect a girl of boosting some rubbers?

Kandi walked into the mart and she spotted an older woman behind the register. She knew the older man who also worked there was gone for a few minutes to get some merchandise so she knew she had to be in and out. She made sure that his black 1995 Honda Accord was out of his designated parking space and after a minute she walked in.

"Hello," the old Asian lady greeted her in broken English. More like "hell" and "oh" were two separate words but Kandi gave her an "A" for effort. At least the woman was trying to lean English.

"Hi," Kandi responded back. She picked up some of the Skittles and Blow Pops she would be paying for and then walked around to where the toiletries were. This store didn't have her brand and to top it off, she did not find the condoms she was looking for. So she figured she'd ask. "Do you have any condoms?"

"Behind counter." The woman said slowly. *Darn*. Kandi thought to her self. She was going to have to pay for the rubbers and figure out a way to boost the candy.

"Okay, I'm going to put these back because I don't have enough money for both." She said as she walked back to the candy aisle and put back the Skittles and Blow Pops and picked up some Airheads and some Lemmonhead and stuffing them in her pocket while reaching for the five dollar bill. "Can I see what kind you have because my boyfriend will only wear a certain kind and I want to make sure I get the right ones?"

"You good." The woman continued her conversation when she seen Kandi make her way to front. "Most men don't wear."

"You right cause if he thinks he's getting anywhere near me without one he'll be by himself."

"Or be wit 'nother woman." The older lady smiled as she put the boxes of rubbers on the table. Kandi cursed herself for not doing a full research. The three pack of condoms cost as much as the twelve packs do at the grocery stores. Oh well, as long as she had some that was what she was most concerned about. She picked out the ones she wanted and the woman rang up her order. "Three dollar and twenty two."

Kandi handed her the five. She looked at the clock next to the exit and realize she had been in the store two minutes too long. She wasn't going to be able grab the bag of chips on the way out unless a miracle happened. Upon receiving her change, she thanked the lady, grabbed her bag and headed towards the door. Just as she was getting ready to walk out the door, the ugliest boy she ever saw walked into here. She immediately dropped her bag and bumped into the chips, pretending she lost balance.

"My fault ma'," the tall young man said as he was helping her up and handing her the bag of chips he thought she dropped. "I didn't even see you."

"Next time watch where you are going, Thing!" Kandi grabbed her bag, the bag of chips and stormed off after calling him a punk. *God must have heard my prayers*, she thought as she said a quick blessing and opened up her bag of chips and continued walking towards her house on Cameron Street. She reached into her pocket and pulled out ten Airheads she managed to swap as well as the box of Lemonheads. She cursed herself for not grabbing something to drink but she didn't expect the conversation to keep her engaged and off her "A" game, and nor did she expect to bump into Thing.

She, along with everyone else she knew at Eldrige Cleaver High School called Josiah Seal "Thing" because the boy looked like a crater face. The pimples were ruining the smooth dark, blue black skin that seemed to match the color of his eyes. But that wasn't the worst part, you could smell him before you could see him. She just didn't know why Thing couldn't just wash his ass everyday just like everyone else. She shook herself and made sure she didn't acquire any of his body odors then she made her way home, happy that even though she didn't get everything she wanted, she got what she needed and that today was a good day.

Chapter 2

"That will be four dollar and forty five," the lady told me when I stepped the counter to pay for my chips and drinks.

"Uh ..." I think my total is incorrect. "My drink was ninety nine cents and the chips were ninety nine cents each. I think my total should be closer to three dollars."

"You gave girl bag of chips and she walk out, you pay for bag of chips." The lady was stern and with a serious look in her face as she held her hand out for my money. "O I call po-po."

That damn Kandi got me. Probably had it planned all along. "Well let me put one of my bags of chips back because my mom is expecting me to bring her back the right amount of change."

The lady didn't look happy about deleting one of the bags from my order. She gave me my change and then she put a bar of soap in a separate bag and she handed the bag for me. "I didn't pay for this." I tried to give her the bag of soap back but she wouldn't take it.

"On da house. Use it. It good for you."

"Thanks," I mumbled.

It was times like this when I hated living in the projects. I can't help it that my mom don't have enough money for us to wash our clothes and that sometimes she puts her hair getting done and her nails right before taking care of my and my baby brother's hygiene. And for the record we don't stink or have bad body odor. Joshua, my little brother, is allergic to certain washing detergents because they make his skin break out in rashes and we can't afford the soap that he needs for his skin. I'd get a job so we could buy the soap but the reality of the situation is, we also can't afford a babysitter so mom depends on me to stay home and handle the family B-I. Well, I do work but I don't want to talk about that now … it's not like I get to keep the money anyway. As for my crater face, I'm not the only one. It just looks like I'm a walking night skyline because my skin so dark. Most of the cleansing stuff they have at the stores irritate my skin and just make it worse. And I can't have my face messed up no more than what it is. But I hit the gym everyday, that's my saving grace right there. I keep my body right cause I can't be fat... face already ugly so I need to have something for the ladies to look at. And since they say nice things about my body from the neck down, it just motivates me to continue pumping the iron when my arms feel like they are going to give or even when my body doesn't want to do it no more. Besides, I have faith that one day, this phase of puberty is going to clean up and that my face is going to clear up and I'm going to have a nice face to set off my six foot one frame.

Eldrige Cleaver High School ain't got nothing but a bunch of haters. That's why I hate coming to this school. I can't believe my mom is making me go to this bap ass school. I would have been doing *fine* at Reynolds High School. I liked the teachers I met there, I had friends going there from middle school, I would have gotten along with people I didn't like and most of all, a negro like me could have had fun. But Cleaver High has everything I don't like.

The first reason I hate this school is because it's an all black school. Naw, scratch that … that ain't why I hate this school. I hate this school because everyone here always run they damn mouth. Spreading gossip and instigating fights, you'd think folks here were trying out for "The Jerry Springer Show." And we wonder why white people and others have problems with us, don't want to help us and always want to take our money. When we're in the classroom, we're the last to enter and the first to leave. We feel have the right to cuss the teachers out and let them say something about us and we call our mamas to come down to the school to act a fool and prove that we are even more niggerish. We got a thousand excuses for why we can't do our work, but we know the words to all the popular rap songs; know who everyone in the entertainment world is beefing with or sleeping with. And damn, must we be loud out the time? I know this is hard, but this is how I see my world. Everyone wants to rock clothes by fashion designers who don't like us, won't hire us and through hip hop, pimp us for the free promotion they don't want from us to begin with. Hell, sometimes, we act just the way they say we act, like a bunch of damn jungle monkeys.

I hate it because we got a bunch of black people who go to this school and they are not upholding this man's memory. We are talking about the man who wrote *Soul On Ice* and was part of a national movement and to thank him at this school that is his namesake, we got these hoochies and hos who try to hit up on every boy they think is cute. They be hanging on them and hugging them every time one walks by. Out of all the guys who go to this school, all the girls want to be date, talk to, be seen with, sleep with or have their name spoken in the same sentence of the same ten or fifteen guys that are popular. And they always going for the athletes, the pretty boys or the class clowns. Regular guys like me don't stand a chance. And these chicks get real extra and go all out of their way to make sure they are noticed. They poke their chest out and shake their behinds but if you slap it, they cuss you out for not treating them like a lady. And then it's the heels ... I don't even know why these chicks are wearing high heels if they can't even walk in them correctly. And the ones not chasing after the flyest guys in school are all about getting them some dude that go to Wake Forest or Winston Salem State. All these girls talking about what college guys ... I meant, child molesters they were dating and what they were going to do to these guys after school. I'm sorry but why are these chicks bragging about giving it up? I thought a girl was supposed to value her virginity but apparently that ain't the case here. I mean, they've taken TLC's "Hat 2 Da Back" to a brand new level; I wish these chicks would put their clothes on I tell ya'. Further evidence that I don't belong here and need to get off of an episode of "In Living Color."

I hate the new school uniforms. For one, the fabric looked cheap and because I'm a young man, my choices were limited. We were only allowed to wear black, gold or white Polos or button up shirts and if we wore the button up shirts, we had to wear a black tie. Black and gold were the school colors and the only reason we were allowed to wear white was because white was considered a traditional dress color. Also, we could only wear black slacks or khakis. The only thing good about this policy was that we could not wear blue or any other color cause I hated blue. Only a busta wore blue so this policy was fine with me. Also, we had to wear black dress shoes. It was in the shoes where we had some real freedom. So whenever you walk into Cleaver we decided that the best way to tell whether or not a dude was serious about his dress in school was if he wore a different pair of shoes everyday. Call me funky if you want to but I did keep a different pair of shoes. Some were older than others but I did the best I could. Oh yeah, before I forget, we had to have belts too and they checked us to make sure our shirts were tucked in and belts were at our waist. If you came to school with your shirt un-tucked, they made you tuck it in. If you wore the wrong color slacks, they made you change into one of the extra slacks that they probably got from some cheap department store. I say hell to the no to that. I will not catch MRSA or any other skin disease that seemed to be going around because I wanted to defy the dress code.

The girls got to wear cute, frilly and fluffy patterns; some that showed off what they were working with above the waist. I liked that because the girls also couldn't wear the Polo's unbuttoned. So if I wanted to draw a picture of one of the chicks at my school and send it to one of my boys in juvie, I could do that because the lines don't lie. The girls also had to wear black or khaki skirts, nude stockings and either flats or heels no higher than two inches. I had to give props to the school board because they looked out for us when they came up with the dress code for the girls, man.

They say the only reason some of us are in this school is because our parents won some lottery. Moms should have talked to me about that cause if it had been up to me, I'd be at a regular, *real* high school. I bet the real reason she sent me to this bama ass school is so she could cover her tracks and make herself look like a *real* parent. This school was supposed to be a mini-college as we worked with professors from the local community college. We stay at this school for five years and then when we graduate, we get a high school diploma and an associate's degree. Sounds like a plan to me.

Anyway, it's another day at this boring school. I'm bored cause quiet as kept, I already know Algebra III and Chemistry. I don't like U. S. History cause all they teach is that black people were slaves, we lost the court case to end segregation and Dr. Martin Luther King, Jr. led the black people to freedom. No disrespect to Dr. King but I know all of this is a bunch of bull. What about the Black Panther Party and the free lunch program? What about how Langston Hughes, Zora Neal Hurston and Richard Wright revolutionized arts in America or how Marcus Garvey encouraged us to consider going back to Africa? Yeah, *his*-story is a bunch of bull cause its only skewed to make white people look like angels and black people to be savages who had to be reformed and civilized. English bores me, not because I hate the language, but I hate the books we have to read. I have sneak in a Donald Goines, Iceberg Slim or Omar Tyree novel to class just so I don't fall asleep and have something to balance out those old American writers I have no respect for or have no interested in learning about. And I get all of this while going to a black school, but I digress.

My motivation for coming to school is that maybe I can get my GPA high enough to get an academic scholarship. Even though Wake Forest is down the street, I got my heart set on UNC. They have a tight law program and I loved the campus. One of my mom's boyfriends took me there the summer before I started at Cleaver and I felt like I was at home. I was around students who wanted to be doctors, lawyers, politicians, business owners; black students who were active at Chapel Hill and their home communities. I even met some guys who were apart of different frats who described growing up in hoods like mine. Though I respect them all, I just knew the black and old gold was the one for me. I felt like I belonged and it was good to know that I wasn't the only person in the hood who was making straight A's and was aspiring to get out.

"That's the thing that bumped into me yesterday," Kandi announced loud Cortez, Kobe and Manuel. I had hoped that I would have run into Hector first instead of dealing with the insane clown posse. "Almost got me caught up."

"Did this dude say excuse me? Or apologize for causing you an inconvenience?" Cortez faked as if he were overly concerned with Kandi's well being. He need to worry about those two babies mamas he got in Kernersville and finding a job rather then being all in my grill about some old news that happened yesterday. As Kandi continued her act, I realized she was killing me softly looking like Lauryn Hill with a perm.

"Yeah, he did," she paused and looked me up and down acting like she was da B-R-A-T, "but he almost blew up my spot. If he hadn't of gave me them chips, it would have been on."

Cortez stepped into my personal space with Kobe and Manuel at his sides. "What you doing mess with my girl dawg?"

I looked him dead in his eye and said, "I wasn't messing with your girl, just like you not going to be messing with me." I balled my fist. "Don't let the geek act fool you brah, just cause I make straight A's don't mean I won't kick your ass." See, to hell with trying to ask him to back off and to leave me alone and shit. These fools always want to bring it to your door step and even though I am a nerd, they need to know that I can, do and will bring it if they step to me.

"You feeling froggy?" He bumped into me trying to trick me into hitting him first so he can claim self defense if we were to end up in the office.

"Jump!" I called his bluff and pulled out my spade card. I was cutting hearts, diamonds and clubs and if they didn't do like Michael Jackson had asked and left me alone, some blood was going to be on the school hall floor. "Ribbit." I wasn't gonna run or scream, but if he hit me, I wasn't gonna stop until I got in enough licks to light up that face.

"Man this punk look like a freckle faced Kermit the frog talking about some damn *ribbit*."

That did it, I swung and if Hector hadn't pulled me back and got in front of me, I would have connected with Cortez. My legs and my fist were ready to jump all over that pond Cortez called a face.

"Move out my way man." Hector was trying to hold me back but Cortez threw his hand at me, rejecting my offer to settle our differences in our ghetto boxing ring.

"I'll catch you in the streets homie." And just like that he walked away and so did the crowd that I didn't even know had gathered around us. I know where that fool stay but I'll meet him on neutral ground so he don't try to ambush me at his house. That's what Manuel did when I showed up at his spot two years ago. He told me some mess about if come to his house if I wanted to get at him and I did. I knocked on the door and he said he'd be out in a minute. I waited on the door to open when I should have been watching my back. Once his brother opened the door, Manuel jumped on me from behind while his brother threw some licks to my chest. I reached back and hit him real good in the nose and then me and his brother got it cracking. I can't say I won the fight but I damn sure didn't lose it. I will say I learned my lesson and at the end of the day, I'll never do that again. I looked at my watch and noticed we had two more classes before school ended. I'd be at the park near our hood complex by the church in about three hours. Hector tried to get my attention by seeing what was on my mind for trying to fight Cortez at school but I didn't have time to listen to all that. I needed to put myself in the zone to rock Cortez' world and every minute between now and then counted.

Chapter 3

This new fight between Cortez and Thing was throwing a monkey wrench in Kandi's plans. She had been scoping out one of the local clothing boutiques on Patterson Avenue for a while now and her plan was to hit the shop up at exactly 4:15 pm. She saw this hot red and black Cross Colours outfit she had to have and the best part was she already had the socks that matched and the shoes at home. Kandi was also pretty sure she or Vickie had some red and black hair accessories that would hold up the look. She had made her appointment with Rajee, this skinny, gay boy who sometimes acted like a girl who lived in two houses from her so she could get her hair braided. Rajee worked fast and always made she was looking right when it was time for her to go to her job. And she hated having to cancel her plans at the last minute because she didn't know when Rajee was going to be able to hook her hair up again and on short notice. She had already paid him his deposit so he could fit her in ahead of a client that already had an appointment with him. Of course, the payment was a new outfit he could sport when he tried to sneak into one of the gay clubs on the south side of town. Now she had to put everything on hold because she had to be there when Cortez rocked Thing's head. She wasn't gonna miss that for the world.

"Hey Kandi," Kandi turned around to see that it was that Janessa Ogsby calling her in the middle of the park all loud and ghetto. Janessa been trying to hang with her ever since she moved to the Tre-4 from Fayettnam ... that's what the kids in North Carolina called Fayetteville because of the

army base and the fact that a lot of people from North
Carolina are sent to there to train. Unlike Kani, Janessa was a
thick girl; cute in the face, thick in the waist. Had the kind of
body that made grown men and young men willing to forget
her age and try to holla at her. "I been trying to catch up with
you. How you been?"

Kandi didn't have anything against Janessa, but she
wasn't a fan of girls. She'd much rather be around Manuel
and Kobe. Speaking of those two, she wondered where they
were at, hoping they'd rescue her from having to entertain
the butterball that was no standing in front of here. "Girl,
I'm waiting to see Thing get his head rocked. Trying to step
to my man like he was some kind of buster, he must be
crazy."

"I know," Janessa jumped in excited. Her face beamed
with joy at the thought of being able to watch the main event
with the girl she wanted to get down with. "This is gonna be
a good fight."

"It's gonna be a straight beat down." Kandi declared as
more of the students gathered at the park to try to get a good
seat. Some of the people got on the swings or stood around
talking. This wasn't an unusual occurrence so the neighbors
or the police that patrolled the area didn't suspect anything
amiss just yet. "It ain't even gonna be a one, two, three. My
man is gonna drop that loser with one punch."

"Hey who taking bets?" Rajee asked all loud and wrong
as he came to the field waving a twenty dollar bill. Rajee
didn't go to school today because he spent the whole day
braiding and perming hair. His mama didn't say nothing like
she usually did when he skipped school to work because with
his father out of the picture, Rajee was pulling his weight and
bringing home the bacon. "I'm trying to double this twenty
and bet on the underdog."

"Un-uh Rajee, how you gonna bet against my man like
that?" Kandi was offended. Rajee's loyalties should have
been with her and her man.

"Girl I'm sorry but uh, I seen Thing naked and he ain't no slouch." Rajee's necked rolled better than any chick Kandi had ever seen. "That boy may be ugly and look like he growing worms out of his face but below the neck, that nigga is fine. And he packing guns. Blair Underwood and Will Smith ain't got nothing on him."

"Cortez is packing guns too," Janessa jumped in before Kandi could fix her lips to defend her man.

"Yeah he packing but Thing's ugly ass been in a few fights and the boy can handle himself." Rajee shut her up and then turned to Kandi, "I'm sorry Boo Boo but everyone is betting on Cortez and the few of us that's got our paper stacked on Thing stand to make a few hundred dollars."

"What's the pot like?" Janessa asked as she and Kandi reached in their pockets and pulled out some Lincolns.

"Fifteen to one in Cortez' favor. But you know Thing will automatically get us our money if Manuel or Kobe jump in it. Then it's gonna be a riot then."

"Don't worry, the homies ain't gonna jump in it unless Thing brings someone to jump in it."

"We still friends right?" Rajee asked Kandi. He didn't want to lose her as a client and actually valued their friendship. She was one of the very few people not quick to call him a fag or make fun of him because of his sexuality.

"Yeah Rajee," of course Kandi wasn't gonna stay mad at the one person in the hood who could do some weave and fix some hair and do it at relatively cheap prices, thus the friendship was mutually benefiting to the both of them ... especially since they both liked bad boys. "Here comes your boy."

Cortez had changed into a gray and blue T-shirt with a matching gray and blue basketball shorts. Manuel and Kobe both were sporting shades of gray and blue as they made their way to the field. The crowd started gathering around, with a few people finding seats at the benches and stuff. Mostly, people stood on the side lines because they knew that anytime folks was gonna get to scrapping, a circle wasn't going to do nothing to contain it. Thing came down the block a few minutes later with Hector at his side. Folks was laughing at him already because Thing was wearing the same clothes he had on when he was at school. Some of the people were holding their noses and claiming they could smell him already.

"Why this dude ain't change clothes?" Janessa wanted to know.

"Cause, dude is just dumb." Kandi had been wondering the same thing.

"Y'all know that boy ain't got no money and that his mama take every dime he get from tricking." Rajee jumped in with no shame airing the boy's dirty laundry.

"What that ugly boy gonna be tricking?" Janessa asked.

Rajee leaned on Janessa's shoulder, "I promise you, he got a thing that be swinging. I've see him in the gym boo, trust me. He ain't that bad from the neck down …. shoot, if he got down with dudes, I'd cover that face up and give him a ride."

Kandi rolled her eyes as she could not believe that Rajee would have a thing for the ugly boy. Cortez and Thing wasted no time getting in the middle of the park, squaring off and throwing blows. To Cortez' surprise, Thing's first punch landed square on the lip and cut it open. Cortez got mad and rushed him and the crowd got excited watching the street fight/boxing/wrestling match. After landing a few face blows of his own, Cortez tried to pick Thing up but couldn't lift him off the ground. Thing took advantage of this and landed a few crucial body blows while Cortez was trying to lift his leg off the ground. When they both fell to the ground, they both rolled around trying to jockey for the dominant position. Before either could get in position, an adult and a police officer broke up the fight.

"Aww man, the po-po come right when the fight is about to get good." Janessa complained.

"Them boys looked like they were having a *different* kind of fight." Rajee threw out there. Janessa looked dumbfounded but Kandi knew what he was trying to say.

"You nasty Rajee ... my man ain't gay." Kandi defended Cortez' honor.

"And you say that like it's a bad thing." Rajee hissed. "I probably could show you a thing or too on how to please a man lil' Miss Virgin." Rajee started looking around the crowd trying to find the guy that was holding their money. "Let's get our money from Demarcus before we have to start another fight. And don't let the fem fool you, I will beat a dude down!" Rajee declared and began to power walk to where Demarcus was posted up on the swings. He quickly turned around and grabbed Kandi's arm and pulled her back a little bit letting Janessa move forward. "We still good on my outfit right? I can fit you in now that the fight didn't happen."

Kandi stepped off the bus rocking the same hair style Cleo rocked in the movie *Set It Off* and that's exactly what she intended to do. She planned to creep like TLC and get in and out undetected. She walked in and was greeted by T-Boz infectious vocals on "If I Was Your Girlfriend" and couldn't resist singing along with the track. At the register was a young Hispanic boy hat looked kind of cute. If she wasn't with Cortez she'd be diggin' on him. She knew that she had caught his eye and that she'd have to flirt with him if she planned on getting in and out with Rajee's stuff. Thank God the boy didn't want much, but still, coming in at 5:15 as opposed to the 4:15 she had planned on was putting a damper on her plans. For a minute, she thought that Rajee might have to drive her to another location.

She went to the men's section and picked out the Polo shirt that Rajee had been talking about wanting to wear at the club this weekend.

"Can I help you?" The pretty boy asked her. The accent was turning her on. She almost felt like she was cheating on Cortez.

"I'm okay. I just wanted to pick some things out for my man."

"Well if you need anything, let me know."

"Okay, thanks."

Kandi had to keep her emotions in check because she wasn't there to pick up a man. She was there to pick up a shirt and a pair of pants and be out. She damned herself for not wearing any glasses. If anything came up missing the boy was going to automatically assume that she did it. She notice another girl coming in baggy clothes, some sunglasses and a baggy purse. If that didn't draw attention, she didn't know what would.

Kandi decide that at the last minute, she was going to try on some clothes instead while she figured out a game plan to get the clothes Rajee had asked for and bounce. She spotted the dressing room and grabbed the pants Rajee asked for on the way in. She put everything down and began attempting to try on the clothes, knowing that the clothes weren't a fit. She exhaled as she looked in the mirror. She really didn't think that this mission was going to go as planned.

As she put on her clothes, she decided at the last minute to wear Rajee's shirt under her own T-shirt and to stuff Rajee's pants inside her own. The shirt was big enough to cover the waist area she hoped and maybe if her flirt game was right, she might be able to snag something else on the house.

After she adjusted the clothing, she walked out and put the extra clothes back and was going to head towards the counter. As she was getting ready to make her way to the counter, the police came in from the back entrance and the woman who was wearing the baggy clothes immediately ran past her and tried to make it out of the front door. Darn. Kandi was trapped.

"Let me go! Let me go!" The big girl complained. The police tried to read her the Miranda rights but the woman was obnoxious and refused to cooperate. Kandi had no choice but to wait the whole situation out and hoped that she wasn't wearing anything that would set off any alarms. She didn't see no cameras so she was confident that no one was going to be able to tell that she had on two sets of clothes.

"That lady is crazy, thinking she gonna steal from us." The pretty boy had approached her as they both watched her being handcuffed and led out of the store. "I knew something was amiss when I saw that baggy outfit and them glasses. It's not that hot for all that."

"Yeah you right."

"But I'm sorry you had to see that though. For your inconvenience, I'll give you this belt for your troubles, it looks like it will go with those pants you are wearing."

"Oh thank you!" She hugged him quickly and let go, she didn't want him to feel Rajee's pants inside her pants. She wrapped the belt around her shirt and thought she looked cute.

"Do you need a ride home? I'm sure my father won't mind me using his car to take you home."

"No that's okay," she lied knowing good and well that she'd have a long wait on the bus and wouldn't make it too far walking without drawing suspicion. But she could not afford the risk of getting caught or being seen in another man's car, especially by Cortez, Kobe or Manuel.

When she heard Outkast rap the lyrics for "Sumtin' Wicked This Way Comes", she knew she had stayed way too long. She walked out and began the journey home. She was *this* close to getting caught and knew she'd have to make better assessments if she wanted to avoid the fate of the woman who left the store before her.

Chapter 4

"Josiah, I swear before God and ten Jesuses that your mother is trifling." Mrs. Sanchez said as she arrived at the precinct to pick me up. I had called my mother but naturally she didn't pick up the phone. I had hoped that Joshua was okay because in my hype to whoop Cortez tail, I forgot to feed him his snack.

"Thank you."

"But what I want to know is what you were doing fighting in the middle of the park? You could have stayed in the house and avoided all this mess with you and that other boy."

She right. I can't even dispute that. Hector did try to talk me out of fighting Cortez but he knew that my mind was set on beating that punk down and that's what I did. After we got arrested, they just finger printed me and then just placed me in a holding cell. Cortez had some priors so he was going to have to post bail.

Mrs. Sanchez probably has acted more like a mother to me than my own. If it weren't for that or the fact that she was Hector's mom, Lord knows I would try to holler. Contrary to popular belief, Hector is black, just as Mr. & Mrs. Sanchez. However when you look at them, you can't tell that Hector is their son. Hector has the same skin complexion as Jurnee Smollett but Mr. Sanchez has bears a slight resemblance to Damon Wayans while Mrs. Sanchez had radiant chocolate looking skin to compliment her shapely full figured body. I bet she and Venus Williams could share dresses. Her long, silky hair and her sleek, chinky eyes makes it easy to compare her to Brandy. I feel guilty thinking about Hector's mom like that, but the truth is the truth and Mrs. Sanchez is a pretty woman. "So what are you going to do to fix this mess?" except when she's mad at me.

"I'll pay you back."

"I'm not worry about the money. I want you to stay out of trouble. You can't go around fighting people every time you turn around." She said as she grabbed my face. She turned my head from side to side and then she let me go. "Your face is getting worse isn't it?"

"Mom!" Hector sounded more embarrassed than I was. I knew my face was getting worse. No matter what I did with what I could do it couldn't be fixed. Every time I could save a dime that I didn't have to give my mother or spend on Joshua, I bought face products with it because lets face it, I know I got a tight body, but I want a tight face too. I'm tired of people calling me Thing. I'd like to be called Josiah for once. Josiah sounds like a name that would be given to man that was handsome and could bed a lot of women ... not a boy who looks like roaches and worms are nesting on his face. I only accept it because I do kinda look like the Swamp Thing.

"Well ... after some of the bruises heal we'll try something else." That's another thing I like about Mrs. Sanchez, she'd always try to find something that would work to help me with my face. I almost wish that she were my mom instead of the one I have now. But Mrs. Sanchez has that kind of affect on people. I've heard that she has a reputation of really caring about the patients that see her in her office. I believe it because I know she really cares about me. "I know of some dermatologists out of Stanford University in California that created a product that may very well work on your skin. They just released it to the market about a year or two ago and I may be able to pull some strings to be able to get you some of the product."

Mrs. Sanchez and I had tried quite a few products but with no success. I believe that if anyone could find me a product that worked on my skin that it would be her. She took us to her house and she left us alone so she could get to her evening client. When I walked into the house, I could see a picture of Hector's older brother with his diploma hanging on the mantle. Hector once told me that the picture was there to remind him of the expectations that he graduate high school, go to college and become successful as he had done and as they had done. Hector's brother had graduated from A & T a year earlier with a degree in mechanical engineering and worked for a firm out in the Midwest. After Hector looked out of the window to make sure that his mom had pulled off the driveway, he came to sit on the couch and turned to me.

"Man, Cortez had an ugly looking face by time you were done with him."

"It's only temporary. In a few days he'll heal and get back to mackin' these girls like he always do."

"You can't think like that Josiah," I had done a double take because I had almost forgotten that that was my real name. Even my mom calls me Thing. "My mom's said she'd find something."

"I know. I just hope that whatever she finds works fast." I exhaled as I flipped back from "Oprah" to catching an episode of "Daria" on the MTV. I'd never confess in public that I liked "Daria." I felt like she and I had so much in common as far as our perceptions of the world. Plus, she was kinda cute. Seeing the jock talking to all the pretty girls only served to remind me of what I was lacking. "At least he'll be able to pick up where life temporarily ended for him."

"Man relax." Hector had moved over to where I'm sitting at. "If anything, I wish I had a body like yours."

"You can't be serious."

"Of course I am. You work hard on it to keep it up. And it's a lot of guys who'd die to have biceps, eight pack and legs like yours. Myself included."

"But what good is a tight body if I scare everyone off with my face? Only reason I work out is so I can work away some of the anger I feel towards other people. Stay out of trouble for the most part."

"I hear you. Maybe I can come to the gym with you."

"Now you want to come?"

"Hey, what can I say? I seen the results of how you handled Cortez and I'm convinced. Besides, I'm already smart, maybe if I bulk up like you, people wouldn't pick on me so."

Hector gets picked on quite a bit, this much I knew to be true. Plus, it would help having someone in the weight room with me so I wouldn't have to go by myself sometimes. Hardly anyone uses the gym equipment when the teams aren't using them and the coach doesn't mind as long as I stay out of trouble. He actually wants me to wrestle for the school but I haven't warmed up to the idea yet. I probably would be good at it but I don't know if I could keep it a sport if someone grabbed on me or felt on me the wrong way, even if it were by mistake. After watching another episode of "Daria" I got up and left so I could check on Joshua. I doubt my mom would be home and someone had to make sure the boy had something to eat.

Chapter 5

Kandi decided to try a new thing ... embracing the femininity that had come over her. She was singing the lyrics to "Kissing You" by this new girl group on Bad Boy Entertainment. After she seen Keisha sporting a skort, which is a skirt with shorts underneath it, she knew she had to have one. Her mother was so pleased to see her wearing the new style that she didn't mind her getting more than one. Her mother was even more shocked to see Kandi go for a real low cut that was similar to Pam's.

After the song went off the radio, she applied her cinnamon colored lip stick with a light brown lip liner. She had already lightly applied the toffee shade blush and three shades of gold and brown eye shadow. On Kandi, the look was natural ... she was wearing makeup without feeling like she sacrificed her tomboy ways. And unlike most girls her age, she wasn't heavy with it.

"So how do I look?" Kandi decided to invite Janessa to her house as she tried on her new look. Even to be a freshman, she had to give Janessa props for not getting carried away with the face powder.

"Girl, I can barely tell that it's there. It looks really good. I didn't think you had it in you."

"Well, sometimes, it's time for a change."

In the two weeks that it had been since she last seen Cortez, he was being forced to spend time on the coast with relatives, she did some investigating. One of the girls carrying Cortez' baby was a girl named Latasha Macy. She was a freshman that has just moved to Kernersville from Cleveland Avenue. To say her parents came up was a true understatement. Latasha had actually approached her when she couldn't find Cortez either and the two struck up a conversation. As it turns out, Latasha wasn't one hundred percent sure that Cortez was even the father because she also revealed that Kobe had sexually assaulted within weeks of discovering that she was pregnant. When Kandi asked why she didn't report it to the police, Latasha told her that Cortez talked her out of it and that Kobe had been paying her hush money through Cortez. Her story was believable to Kandi because she remembered a few tense incidents between the Kobe and Cortez a few months back that they would not discuss in front of her or Manuel.

It was Latasha that told her about the other girl, Meonna. Her nickname was Loose Lips because her specialty was sinking ships if you catch the drift. Latasha had told Kandi that she had one conversation with Meonna just so they could get along in the event that both of their babies were by Cortez. The meeting didn't go well because Meonna wanted her girls to jump Latasha for the sole reason of making her loose her baby. After that confrontation, another guy at the school she went to had confided in her that Meonna had told another guy that the baby was his and when Cortez had found out that Latasha had went snooping, he cussed her out and denied the baby being his.

Even with all this information, Kandi was willing to put all this aside to be with Cortez. At least she knew where he had been and he was definitely not getting anywhere near her without a latex barrier. She had heard of Loose Lips before because she over heard some of the guys on the football team bragging about how they made her an "initiation requirement" for the new guys on the team ... whatever that meant. Kandi had decided that she could deal with Latasha and her baby as long as Latasha knew her role and didn't try to role up on her man. Hell, she'd even be the baby's Godmama just so she could get in good with Cortez. She was a true ride or die chick and was willing to accept Cortez flaws and all.

After Kandi finished getting dressed, she called Cortez to let him know that she was ready for their date. She had been so excited when she found out that Cortez was going to be back that she immediately suggested that they watch *Boyz N Da Hood* and *Inkwell* at his house while his mom was away at work. Cortez had honked the horn twice when he arrived and Kandi and Janessa rushed to the door. Kandi made sure the rubbers she had bought a few weeks ago were secure in her pocket. She didn't want there to be no excuses for why he couldn't use one. She also wasn't trying to get pregnant. Janessa coyly waved at Cortez and walked home. Kandi got in on the passengers side of the vehicle. They looked at each other and shared a kiss.

"I see you've morphed into a beautiful butterfly while I was away."

"You don't look too bad yourself pretty boy." Kandi smiled and flirted back. "Beside every man there's a bad girl." She quoted a verse from Lil' Kim's rap.

"I know." Cortez put his hand on her leg for a while and then pulled off. On the way to his place, he was listening to *The Show, The Afterparty, The Hotel* by Jodeci. To be such a thug, Cortez was a still a Jodeci fan. He liked them because they were hardcore guys who dressed and acted like rappers but could sing like church boys. Plus, he wasn't a punk for bumping their hard beats in the bass in his car. Cortez had stopped at Burger King and got them both fish sandwich combos with Sprites.

When they got out of the car, she watched him as he led the way to his crib with their food in his hand. He looked so damn sexy, she never realized how broad his shoulders were or how muscular his arms looked from her angle. She made sure to grab the bags of food while he unlocked the door.

Upon stepping inside, she heard Maxwell playing in the background, bragging about how he was going to keep going until the cops came knocking. Kandi didn't want no cops or anyone else interrupting her night. Cortez had laid out a blanket in the middle of the floor and pushed the sofa, loveseat and the coffee table back so they could have more room.

"I would have set this up in my room, but the bed squeaks when you move on it and I don't want my nosey neighbors telling my mom's all my business."

"No problem."

The television in the living room was bigger than the one on Cortez' room anyway, so Kandi was cool with that. They sat down and said blessings and ate their dinner before it got cold. Cortez pressed play on the remote so they could watch *Inkwell.*

"So why the change?" Cortez asked after they were almost done with their meal. "This is the first time I remember you showing your figure."

"I finally found something I feel comfortable wearing." Kandi lied. She hadn't gotten used to seeing so much of her skin or that her girls were out. But she did like the outfit and figured she could get used to wearing it. "Besides, I can still play ball or just chill with the fellas."

"But you can't wear that." Cortez got defensive. "You should only wear that sexy hood chick outfits around me."

"I can do that."

"But can you do this?" Cortez leaned in and kissed her. *Yes* she exclaimed with excitement. She and Cortez were going to finally go at it and she felt great. She pulled off his new Kobe Bryant Laker's jersey and admired how defined he looked below the neck. Cortez had pulled her top off and was kissing on her nipples in a frenzy while working his fingers up her skort. These sensations and feeling were new to Kandi and she liked them. Cortez started to pull her skort down but Kandi hesitated.

"What's wrong?" Cortez asked. Kandi wanted to respond but couldn't find the words to escape her lips. "Oh I get it." Cortez stood up and dropped the jersey shorts. Kandi was mesmerized at what she saw and started getting apprehensive about her ability to satisfy Cortez. There was no way he was going to stick all of that in her. Cortez got on top of her and started kissing her again. "I'm not going to hurt you." He whispered in her ear and work her skort down. Feeling him on her started feeling real good as they rolled around on the floor and kiss. When Cortez got Kandi in the missionary position, he reached for his pants and pulled out a condom. He sat up, tore the package, pulled it out and unrolled it on his member. Kandi was surprised that the latex was able to stretch and accommodate him fully. Cortez kissed Kandi again and slowly began to inch his way inside. Kandi tensed up and resisted his urges.

"No I can't do this." Kandi tried to get away.

"What do you mean no?" Cortez questioned. "I promise to go slow and make this as less painful as possible."

Cortez kissed Kandi again and once he felt she was comfortable he again tried to be the first to enter inside her. Kandi felt him pushing in and as much as she wanted to, her body was telling her no.

"I can't do this." Kandi cried as she pushed Cortez off of her. "Please get off of me."

"Aw hell, come on!" Cortez was understandably angry.

"I'm not ready for this."

"Then get out!" Cortez said violently. He stood up and pulled Kandi up. Kandi reached for her skort and pulled it up. She barely got her top on good before Cortez grabbed her arms and her shoes and threw them both out of his house.

A dark chocolate hand reached up and got a firm grip on my left pec as I sat at the head of the bed with the sheets barely covering my body. The smooth, glittering peaches and cream nail polish began to shine and sparkle in the bright moonlight and had distracted me from the task at hand. I had been focused on carefully unrolling the latex the lady and

I had been using so I could discard it. I had been feeling around and making my visual inspection to make sure that nothing came out that wasn't supposed to come out if you get my drift. Upon satisfaction that I had another successful tour with my brand of choice, I began to wish that Janita was as careful as I was. I wrapped it and the wrapper up in a paper towel and began to plan my exit. We were done.

"You want to go for another round baby?" The lady sat up and asked. I looked at the digital clock with its red light beaming the time back to me. Not to be rude but a brother had to go. I had a long day today and staying and spending the night would only make the day longer than it needed to be. "You cleaned up nicely. What your mom got you using?"

"A friend hooked me up with some Proactiv Solution. Been using it for a few weeks now ... I'm happy that the pimples and the face blemishes are gone."

"Me too, now I can look at that pretty face of yours instead of your mother making you wear that bag over your head."

I was nervous about how I'd look when I met the trick for my appointment. I have no idea how much she paid my mom to spend the night with me. I don't even remember her name and she's a regular. I have no idea where my mom found these ladies, but all she said was that they were paying top dollar to be with a young man in the privacy of their own home. I have no idea what my mom called top dollar because Joshua and I never saw it. But moms always had her hair did and nails done and some expensive clothing like the ones I seen in the VIBE magazines.

"I'm good ... I'll see you around probably the end of the week." I had reached over and started looking for my clothes. There was enough light creeping in from the windows because the shades were turned up all the way, but that was cool. I could feel the girl pulling at me and trying to turn me on while convincing me to stay.

"I don't think I can wait till the end of the week Cortez ..." Before I could think straight I glared at her. No she didn't just call me by another dude's name, especially that fool's name. Damn it! I've definitely picked up the pace and began pulling up the pants and putting the shirt on at the same time. True, I didn't remember this woman's name but I was going to save face by not putting that out there. If she didn't remember my name, she could have at least played it off or just kept the conversation general. "No I'm sorry Josiah, I meant Josiah."

I'm sure she did. She was sorry that she wasn't going to be able to get the piece of me she wanted inside of her again.

"Naw baby, you spoke what your heart felt."

"But Cortez can't even rock it like you. He's not as big as ..." I had begun to tune her out because out of the abundance of the heart the mouth speaks and this chick had a thing for some dude named Cortez ... hopefully not my enemy Cortez but a Cortez all the same. I had opened the door and I suddenly felt a wave of rejection and disappointment because for the whole hour we had shared our bodies and worked to make sure both of us got something good, I was not on my job cause she called me by another dude's name. I even tried to figure out what I could have done differently but on the real, I'm not going to sweat it too much longer because I would probably never see her again in her bedroom and if I did, she would get another shot at the kid again. "Josiah don't leave out here like this."

I turned my head to glance at her. Damn, she was sexy ... just like a darker version of Taj from SWV. Shaped like her too and even had the long silky hair. She was still topless even though she had a sheet up to her neck covering her figure. I shook my head in disappointment and walked out of the door. I put my hand in my right pocket and pulled out the balled up paper towel that had what could've been hers if she were that special one I wanted to be with. Fortunately for me on the next block there was a corner store and a trash can so I could discard the memory of a bad time.

Everyone says sex is supposed to feel good and when you get that release you are supposed to feel good. Why didn't I feel that way now? I mean, besides the obvious of the chick calling me the wrong name, how come I didn't feel like I just had the best thing since sliced bread? The whole purpose of getting undressed and having fun is so I could feel good about it in the end. Maybe if my introduction to sex had been nobler I wouldn't feel this way.

My mother pawned my virginity to this street hooker when I was twelve. She had the nerve to say it was my fault because if I hadn't of walked behind the building to take a leak that I probably could have waited to get into the house and do, she wouldn't have seen my "meat." The hooker wasn't ugly but I would not have chose her to do it with if it were up to me. I don't know too much of the particulars behind how it all went down, but I do know that she paid my mom $150 to be the first one to take my manhood on a test drive. And the whole time I was with her I was uncomfortable because when she put it in her mouth, it tickled and was slightly discomforting because I felt her teeth. I didn't want to hit her in the face because if she had bit my stuff I would have caught a case, for real. Then the chick guides it in and just bouncing up and down and moaning and groaning and sounding like I'm hurting her or something.

To make matters worse, my perverted ass mom was standing at the doorway, videotaping the entire thing. While I'm trying to figure out what the hell I'm doing and how I could possible get something out of the whole ordeal of being butt naked and sticking my thing in an older woman's twat, she's over here coaching and shouting at me as she were a proud father at one of my baseball games. At the time, I had heard about sex and even seen grown folks do it in a couple of R-rated movies, but I barely had enough hair on my private area to be getting down like that. And just like a proud father, she called some of his girls when it was over, had some drinks while I had a can of Coke and they replayed the whole thing as if it were Monday Night Football. I was so angry and embarrassed but what could I do? Then one of her friends was saying how she'd pay anything to be a young man and that gave her the idea to pimp me out.

A few days later, I had to be taken to the clinic because my penis wouldn't stop burning when I took a leak and my joint smelled like a yeast and fish experiment gone haywire. The smell was so pungent that I thought it reeked from my jeans. Dark grayish and black bumps that looked like molded cauliflower rose up like pimples at the head and were irritated every time the fabric from my underwear rubbed up against it. I was scared to touch it because I didn't want whatever it was to get on my hands and work its way to my other two hundred parts. Moms wasn't too pleased with that.

So what did I get out of my mother pawning my virginity? A first hand experience with an STD from some semi fine chick, a trip to McDonalds for a combo meal that my mother thought would make up for the whole ordeal and a Michael Jordan jersey set. And now my biggest problem

Kandi hadn't spoken with Cortez since that night when she failed to give Cortez her virginity. Everytime she called to try to talk things over Cortez would either hang of the phone or ask his mom to lie and say he wasn't home when he was. She spotted the crew at lunch and decided to make her presence known.

"What's up my nig …"

"Nothing's up trick." Cortez said coolly. Kandi hadn't been expecting that and even though she kept a straight face, Cortez' words hurt her to the core.

"Why I got to be a trick?"

"Cause you play games." Cortez said as Kobe and Manuel continued to eat and not look her way. "One minute you want to give it up and the next minute you yelling stop."

"Well you know I don't give it up like that." Kandi said trying to sit next to him and talk some sense into him.

"Naw, you don't give it up at all." Cortez pushed Kandi out of her seat and stepped over her. "I need a ride or die chick for real and you not ridding no more." Cortez yelled. Everyone stopped eating their lunch and looked at Kandi. She got up and walked out of the cafeteria pretending like her feelings weren't hurt. She walked behind the building and when she was sure that no one had found her, she began releasing her tears.

Chapter 6

As I looked into the mirror, I was happy at the results. After three weeks, my pimples and facial blemishes were almost gone. I almost looked like I had a baby face. I could smile and be pleasantly pleased at the reflection looking back at me. Mrs. Sanchez really looked out for me. I finally see what I guess she saw in me all along.

I put on my clothes and made sure Joshua was taken care of before I walked out of the door to go to school. After walking a few blocks, I met up with Hector.

"Wow! That stuff my mom got you really works. You really look like a new person."

"I feel like a new person."

"Watching you use the products and slowly but surely the pimples and the blemishes were disappearing before my eyes. That is what's up?"

"Yeah, and I have to admit, that soap the lady at the convenience store gave me worked wonders too. It doesn't irritate my skin and Joshua can use it. She said it was all natural and homemade and that she'd give me the recipe the next time I go in there. She agreed to show me how to make it so I could take care of myself better. She even suggested some of the body oils that would work well with my skin."

I definitely feel like I had arrived. I never been the conceited type but man oh man, do I feel good this morning. When Hector and I walked on the campus, all the eyes were on us. Hector had been working out with me for the past few weeks too and although he's not going to get a frame overnight, he's at least carrying that heavy backpack better.

"Thing is that you?" A girl who I don't even remember where I knew her from asked me.

"My name is Josiah."

"Oh, you're a new kid."

I can't believe this girl was trying to play me like I was brand new. Everyone knows that Hector and I been tight since we got to this joint.

"Naw, folks used to call me Thing. They call me Josiah now."

I want to cuss her out. Her mannerisms remind me of one of those uppity chicks that always thought they were too good for someone. She thought cause she had some weave and some hazel contacts that she was automatically a dime. Instead I just pushed passed her with Hector in tow and headed to our lockers. We had Algebra III today so my mind needed to be focused on learning some of these equations and being able to work through them problems and not some skank who is getting over her temporary amnesia and now all of a sudden wants to get with me.

"Thing!" Janessa shouted. People continued to gawk and stare as we approached our lockers. "You got to tell me your secret. I know a girl who can use whatever you are using to clear your skin. I didn't know you was hiding all of that under there."

"A lot of people didn't know." I told her after put in the combination to my lock. "Most of the people at this school treated me so horribly because I didn't look like a pretty boy or because I wasn't popular. Now all of a sudden folks want to treat me like I'm the best thing since slice bread."

Janessa and I looked at the girls who were at nearby lockers who were giggling and talking about how fine I was and talking about hooking up with me.

"I'm sorry if you felt I was that way," Janessa said sincerely, or at least I thought it was sincere. I couldn't tell. Even though she'd look like she never miss her meal or mine, she'd still seems like the chick that would point at me and laugh if she had the opportunity.

"I'm good. It's your conscious you have to answer to at the end of the day. I know I never did wrong by nobody and I'm not gonna let my new looks quote unquote change who I am now."

I noticed Rajee coming to his locker and throwing his book bag in there like he was mad or something. I didn't really have anything against the guy but because he was homo, I didn't exactly associate with him that much either. But I will admit, when everyone was calling me Thing, he was one of the few that called me Josiah and was at least cordial with me. "What's up Rajee?" I could at least find out what's wrong with the guy and get him to calm down or something. I had hoped that he wasn't mad at no girl because I'd have to restrain him. He may act like one but that don't give him the right to hit one.

"When I see Cortez, Kobe or Manuel, I'm gonna kick they ass!"

"What they do to you?" Hector beat me to the punch.

"They over here lying saying that they had some kind of three way with Kandi and I know she don't do things like that." Rajee was heated. I never see the boy jump up and act like that. "Then gonna try to play her in the cafeteria yesterday and taunt her after school."

"Now you know you can't fight Cortez and Kobe and Manuel not jump up in that."

Rajee rolled his neck, two of his eyes and snapped, "I *want* Kobe and Manuel to jump up in this. I *want* them to jump in this here. They'll be catching a trip to 1226 10th Avenue, I'll Beat They Ass, North Carolina. Don't let this gloss and these nails fool you. I'm a thug honey and them sissies can get it."

At that moment I seen Kandi walking to her class. I shut my locker and followed her. I didn't know if Rajee was just mad or needed to blow off some steam but right now, I just needed to get to Kandi.

"Kandi wait up!" I yelled. I had over heard some girls who were walking to class pass along the same rumor that Rajee just told me and I thought that was a punk move for the dudes to be talking about some girl like that. Especially a girl who I know has rode for them and their cause plenty of times and dealt with females who were a problem.

"Just leave me alone Thing!"

"Look at me," I grabbed her arm and turned her around. Instinctively, she wanted to hit me but I blocked her shot. "Just give me a chance to talk to you."

"What do we have to talk about?" Kandi was angry and I could tell she was trying to hold some tears back.

"I just want you to chill so you don't do nothing stupid."

"What am I supposed to do Thing?" She finally looked at me and exhaled. She shook her head because I don't think she thought she was talking to me. "It's me, Thing."

"You look different."

"Yeah, but lets talk about you."

"I can't believe Cortez, Manuel and Kobe would stab me in the back after all I done for them. All the girls who got their asses whopped at my hands just because they said jump. All the times I covered for them when they were doing their dirt and this is how they treat me. They tried to make me into some whore."

"Look, I know you are not a whore." Trust me, I knew from personal experience. "You know you are not a whore and they know you are not a whore."

"He just saying that cause I won't give him none. He done already been with half of Winston anyway, and he got one maybe two girls pregnant. I can't believe I used to like him."

Before I could comfort Kandi some more, I could here Rajee yelling down the hallway. "Say that to my face! Say that to my face! You wasn't calling me no fag when I was sucking …" and before I could figure out who Rajee was talking too, the crowd was in pandemonium. We started to break so we could go see who was fighting but that wasn't even necessary. Rajee and Kobe were tussling in our locker area trying to throw each other against the way. Rajee was trying to break free so he could punch Kobe in the head but Kobe's grip was too strong. I decided to break it up because I knew that Manuel and Cortez were not too far behind and we weren't in our hood and that they wouldn't hesitate to break Rajee off at school just to humiliate him. They wasn't gonna let no homo show them up. Kandi pushed Rajee back while Hector and I had a grip on Kobe.

"Let me go man."

"Go back to your class and stop lying on Kandi."

"Whatever fool." Kobe pushed us away, dusted himself off and walked back to his class. Rajee had calmed down but he was walking towards the office with one of the assistant principals. I went to where Kandi was so I could make sure she got to her locker and headed back to her class. When Kandi and I turned around, we could see Cortez and Manuel grilling us. I returned the same grill and dared them to come close to us. Cortez balled and unballed his fist and he grabbed Manuel and pulled him away from the crowd. I made sure Kandi made it to her first period and I promised to meet up with her at the start of second period.

Chapter 7

Kandi hated coming to school. Everyday for the past week everyone just looked and stared at her when she walked by. She could hear the other students whisper and only bold would point and laugh at her behind her back. But even they made sure they were at a safe distance when they did so.

"I know you're not a whore," Janessa assured her. Through it all, Janessa had been one of the few students who was there for her, who'd speak to her and look her in the eyes while doing so. "You know how boys are, they lie on their penises all the time." She was trying to cheer Kandi but as she was the past week, she was unsuccessful at getting her to smile today. "I bet you if you went around and told everyone how small their penises were you probably could turn this around real quickly. And if you need pictures, girl, I got you."

That brought a smile to Kandi's face. "You are a mess." She chuckled for the first time in a week. Janessa had finally gotten through to her. "What are you doing with pictures of naked dudes anyway?"

"Have you heard of the internet?" Janessa asked because she knew that everyone wasn't as fortunate as her to have an AOL account or in her case, her own screen name. When Kandi didn't respond, "well, you know I want to be a journalist and I'm still trying to get on the school paper. I don't know why they don't let freshman be apart of the school paper but I digress. Anyway, if Cortez, Kobe or

Manuel feel froggy I can give them something to make them jump, you know."

"Thanks Janessa." Kandi had started warming up to the idea of having Janessa around. Wasn't like she had a choice. They walked past Cortez and the crew on their way to their classes. Manuel whistled on the sly and the three boys laughed. Kandi stopped in her tracks and turned around as opposed to ignoring them like she had been doing. Before she could think of something to say, Janessa had walked up to Manuel and put her hands on her hips.

"You must got the game twisted if you think you are going to catch a girl like that."

"You turned around," Manuel responded, "you must have understood your call." That made the boys laugh some more.

"Janessa come on," Kandi walked up to Janessa and tried to nudge her friend along. "These boys aren't even worth it."

"You're right, they're not." Janessa said as she pretended to walk away. Once Kandi had gotten a head a few steps, Janessa turned right back around walked up to Manuel and hauled off and slapped the taste out of his mouth. Manuel wanted to retaliate but Kandi grabbed Janessa and stood in front of her.

"So you gonna hit a girl now?" She challenged. "I remember when it was my job to take care of the chicks for you. But I tell you something else, hit me or Janessa and I'll beat you like the punk you are." Manuel got in her face and Kandi looked over to where Cortez and Kobe were standing around watching what was gonna happen next. "Y'all some punks. Gonna let your boy swing on a girl."

"You used to roll with dudes," Cortez said nonchalantly, "you can get beat like one."

"You little bitch!" Manuel pushed Kandi and Kandi and Janessa pushed Manuel back. Each of them socked Manuel in the jaw. Manuel reached up to punch Kandi and his fist was caught in the air by Hector. Manuel and his boys were caught by surprise but they also looked around because they knew Thing wasn't too far behind.

"You want to settle this mano y mano?" Hector challenged, wanting to get a piece of Manuel himself.

"That's alright." Manuel wrestled his wrist away from Hector. "Your day is coming chica. You can bet on that."

Manuel walked past his boys and headed off to his class. The crowd dispersed, disappointed that they didn't get to see another fight.

"Thank you," Kandi said to Hector, "you didn't have to jump in that."

"Yeah I did." Hector cut her off, "no man should be bold enough to put his hand on a girl. It's bad enough they are lying about you but to strike you, I couldn't watch that and not do nothing about that."

They both hugged Hector and kissed him on the cheek. Hector smiled as he and Janessa walked arm and arm into their first period class. Kandi's class was down the hall so she picked up the pace so the late bell wouldn't ring.

Kandi decided to thank Hector by getting him a fly shirt or two he can wear every now and then. Hector always looked like he was Steve Urkel's little brother with them glass and the pens and pencils in his front pocket. Janessa's investigating skills had come in handy when she came up with Hector's shirt size. She didn't know whether those two had something going on or not but she did want to look out for him as he did for her. She had looked for Thing that day too but didn't see him. She had heard that he had been sick a few days ago but didn't follow up on that.

Kandi stood in front of the entrance to another neighborhood clothing store. She felt weird in a black tie-dyed Notorious B. I. G. shirt with baggy jeans. She looked in the mirror and just knew the look didn't compliment her current hairstyle. *I should have worn a hat,* she thought but she knew she wouldn't have this opportunity again. Business was moderate, enough for her to get in and get out. She quickly spotted the two shirts she wanted and went over the plan in her head on how she was going to get the shirts out of the store. What she hadn't counted on, was Manuel bumping into her when she turned around.

"I see you don't have your little tortillera with you."

"Whatever." She started to put down what she was going to get but decided against it. If nothing else, she may be able to use Manuel as a distraction of some sort. Plan A and Plan B were out the window so she had no choice but to improvise, but that would prove to be risky. So she decided to abort the mission "Aren't Cortez and Kobe looking for you?"

"Naw, they know I'm gone."

"Oh," Kandi decided not to stand around and entertain a conversation with him. She put the shirts back and decided to walk out of the store. She was almost at the door when strong hand grabbed her arm and jerked her away. She looked up into the face of an older Hispanic guy who looked like he spent a few years in the pen.

"I believe you have something that belongs to us." He said in perfect English to Kandi's surprise.

"I believe you made a mistake. I have nothing that belongs to you and I changed my mind about buying those two shirts over there when that boy over there started harassing me."

"Harassing you. Chica please. If anything, I was trying to help you save face so my uncle wouldn't catch that wallet you'd boosted from him when you came in the store."

"I didn't boost no wallet," but Kandi's pleas went unanswered as the man searched and violated her body. He succeeded in pulling out the wallet she didn't even know was in her front pocket. She glared at Manuel as she realized she had set her up. Had to give him props, the guy worked fast to slip the wallet into her pocket without her knowing about it. "I didn't take your wallet sir, Manuel must have put it in my pocket when he bumped into me."

"She's lying."

"I don't know if I can believe you." The man said, "my wallet was in your front pocket. Besides, you may not have boosted this wallet that magically appeared in your front pocket, but you've stolen from me before."

"Yeah, you did," she turned to the direction of the voice and seen the familiar pretty boy who she had flirted with weeks ago. "This is the girl that got us for one of our Cross Colours outfits a few weeks ago." He got in her face only this time he wasn't smiling or flirting with her. "It's a shame because I never pegged this pretty girl to be a thief."

"She's a lot of things you don't know about." Manuel slipped.

"Shut up!" Kandi screamed as she fought the uncle to let go of his grip so she could confront Manuel.

"Is there a problem?" A Hispanic police officer came into the shop and she knew that her problems were just beginning.

Chapter 8

Me and these dreamy eyes of mine were not trying to wake up. I had been sick for three days and now it was time to go to school. The jonz in my bonz had me fiending for a lady like the one D'Angelo was singing about when the alarm went off. The phone had ringed at the same time and I picked it up. I knew it couldn't be nobody but Hector.

"Hey man, you coming to school today?"

I was right.

"Yeah, I'll be there. I got to get Joshua ready. You know that boy don't want nobody touching him or working with him in the morning. He's worse than a girl."

Hector laughed on the other end. "I'll be there in about ten minutes. I got some things I want to show you."

"I'm not trying to think about no school right now. I can wait til I get there."

"Naw, we got Algebra III first and the teacher dropped some stuff on us that you need to be prepared for. I tried to call you yesterday but your mom about chewed my head off thinking I was one of those floozies who been calling for her son."

My phone had been blowing up since my skin cleared up, for real. It was off da hook like an Xscape album. And the messages they were leaving had me feeling so good, until I thought about how some of these same chicks wouldn't give me the time of day at the end of the year. And these were some bold chicks who did not care whether or not I had my own line or not. I almost felt sorry for some of these girls who were getting cussed out. But then again, this was my mama's fault too because she was the one who thought it would be a good idea to get the phone bill in my name.

Hector kept his word and showed up ten minutes after getting off the phone with me. I had just gotten Joshua out of the shower so I could get his clothes on. After I open the door, I took down some bowls from the cupboard so I can pour us some cereal.

"When was the last time you talked to Kandi?"

"Last day I was at school. What's up?"

"I heard she got busted boosting some clothes from Manuel's uncle's shop. I also heard Manuel bragging about how he set her up."

"Word?"

"Yeah man, by the lockers. They were snickering and carrying on about how she was the new ride or die bandit."

"I didn't know that Manuel had it in him to snitch. I'm surprised that Kobe and Cortez would go for that."

"We'll see. But let me show you this problem that we had for homework yesterday."

Looking at the problem, I can say I had never seen so many variables and exponents before in my life. This looked like one of those formulas Albert Einstein or somebody like that would be able to solve in their sleep. I gave the paper back to Hector, wasn't no use in keeping this in my hands.

"Josiah, you didn't even look at it."

"Yes I did. The only thing I can tell you is that seven cubed equals three hundred and forty three. The rest we need help with."

"Man, I'm mad you knew the answer to that without a calculator."

"I wasn't getting into UNC on my mesmerizing looks and my captivating beauty."

Hector laughed at my silliness and when Joshua was done, I took his bowl and spoon and put it in the sink. I took a few bites out of my cereal and then I washed the dishes that were in the sink from last night and put them in the drainer before heading out of the door.

I looked all over the school for Kandi but I did not see her. Folks are gossiping about how she got caught boosting and claiming that they knew what kind of time she was going to do. I have never been one to listen to all that gossip anyway. Of course, now I have an interest in what was being said because so many girls had been lying on my mini me and claiming I had been with them on such and such a night when I was in home in the bed puking my brains out … at least it felt like that was what I was doing.

I stepped out of the school and I could hear the Bad Boy Remix to Gina Thompson's "The Things You Do" booming from one of the football jock's car. The infectious symbols and drum beat had the girls nodding their heads on the way to the bus stop.

"Look who decided to come to school." I could hear that punk even though the song was loud and I was several feet from him.

I faced Cortez for the first time in a week and now, I have no idea why I was jealous of this dude in the first place. As I walked over to where he stood, I realized he wasn't as perfect as I thought he was. I seen a few pimples pop up on his forehead. Too much of that greasy pizza and ketchup and ranch dipped fries if you ask me. Can't talk about him cause I used to eat that mess too.

"I'm here, what's up?"

Cortez looked at me like he had seen a ghost and then straighten up real quick to save face. "Man wasn't nobody talking to you."

"But you were talking about me what's up?" I didn't have time to play games with this fool. And if a rematch was what he wanted, he could get his grill knocked in a school. I could benefit from another few days off from school.

"Look, you need to be up out of my face."

I stepped closer. I was never one scared of a challenge.

"Naw, don't fight man. He ain't worth it." Hector stepped up and pushed me aside from Cortez. Kobe had grabbed Cortez and pulled him on to the bus. One of the girls who had been watching from the sidelines came up to me and asked for my number. She crazy. I can't think of my seven digits right now and I wouldn't give them to her if I did. "You and Cortez are never gonna stop fighting are you?"

"I wouldn't say that," I readjusted my backpack on my back started the walk home. "As long has he knows to stay in his lane and stay out of mine, we won't have any beef."

"Yeah, but y'all been bumping heads a lot lately. I'm just worried about you."

"Aww," I grabbed Hector's head, put it under my harm and gave him a noogie. Hector got out of it and pushed me away. As we kept walking, he seen Kandi sitting on the porch. "Yo, you go ahead, let me talk to Kandi for a minute."

"Peace."

I walked to where Kandi was sitting and I sat down next to her. I looked in her eyes and she quickly turned away.

"Why you go and do that?"

"Cause I know you ain't even trying to holla at me like that. You probably got some jokes for me too." Kandi got madder and then she got in my face. "Say something smart and I'll beat the ugly back in you."

"That's not the way to talk to me yo'" I sat up thinking it was a mistake to try to talk to her. "You know I haven't been in school for a few days so I don't know anything about what folks are saying about you."

"I'm gonna kick Manuel's punk faggot ass, you can believe that."

"What he do?"

"The little bastard set me up. That's alright though."

"Man forget them fools. All they do is pick on folks who they think are weaker than them and don't stand up for themselves."

"I used to be like that." Kandi's confession had surprised me. "I thought I was better because I didn't hang with girls and get into all the gossip and stuff but picking fights with other females and acting like Cortez and I were in a relationship when he was *clearly* cheating on me and sleeping with any girl who'd give him some didn't make me any better."

I wrapped my arm around her, "look at it like this. You used to do those things and you *used* to do anything to please Cortez. Now that you got rid of that dead weight, you can do what's right for you, not what's good for that fake ass crew."

Kandi shook her head, "but I still got to go to court and try to beat this case. I know I'm wrong for boosting and all, but I can't go to juvenile and be traveling all over the state like Vickie. Plus, I didn't boost nothing that time."

"But you had before?" I didn't know that was Kandi's side hustle. All this time, I thought the girl had a little dough or that Cortez was hitting her off. I didn't know her five fingers did the tricks for her. "You got a second chance to make things right. If this is your first time getting caught, maybe the judge will have some leniency on you. Especially if they can prove you were set up."

"Well, according to Manuel's uncle they got me on film putting the clothes on in the dressing room. I hope they got Manuel on film slipping the wallet in my pocket."

"So where did the clothes end up?"

"I gave them to someone in exchange for some services."

"I see." It's not like I could have hooked her up or something. "Can I ask you something?"

"What's up?"

"What's really up with you and Cortez?"

"That bastard be lying on me. Ever since I punked out and didn't give him none, he been making up stories about what I did to him and his crew and how he had me screaming and what kind of freak I am."

"You and Cortez never had sex?" I couldn't believe it. I knew for sure that Cortez was hitting that because I don't know too many girls who would turn Cortez down. I had heard about how he be doing his thing with the girls often from the girls themselves.

"No, I wanted to but when the time came, I couldn't do it. It's not that I didn't think he was sexy but I'm a virgin and I just wasn't ready."

I never thought I'd hear a girl in my class say she was a virgin. I'm not saying all of them are hoes, but a lot of them give up the panties by time they are in high school. Quiet as kept, even I have had a sampling of the girls at school ... but it's always been on the low. Most of the girls that got with me wanted to find out if I could do the do in the bedroom cause they heard it from someone who knew someone who paid my moms to do me. If my mom knew what I was doing behind her back I'd never hear the end of it.

"Well, maybe you need a man who is willing to wait until you are ready."

I do like Kandi, flaws and all. As long as she don't try to steal nothing from me then we can still be cool.

"Yeah, maybe that's what I need."

Kandi laid her head on my shoulder and we looked out on the porch and talked about every car and person that walked by. Joshua and some of his friends played at a nearby house so I always had my eye on him. Moms is paging me letting me know that she had something set up but I just wasn't up for it today. It ain't like Joshua and I were going to see the money anyway. I needed to find a way to be strong and tell her I wasn't gonna trick no more, but right now, sitting next to Kandi is giving me all the strength I needed.

Chapter 9

Kandi missed the bus. Not because she wanted to, but due to the terms of her probation and restitution, she was ineligible to go on the junior class trip to Carowinds. Instead, she worked with the janitors at school cleaning up behind the freshman and sophomores where cleaning out their lockers and taking final exams. The seniors had graduated the day before and were already gone from campus.

"Is there some extra gloves around this joint?" Kandi was shocked to hear Janessa walking to the locker area where she was throwing loose papers in the trash. Janessa was looking like the clean up woman in her florescent pink scarf that was doing a horrible job concealing the rollers in her hair, a faded Kris Kross t-shirt and some sweat shorts.

"What are you doing here?" Kandi asked because she didn't want the head janitor, Ms. Carter, going back to tell her probation officer that she was socializing during her community service time.

"Girl, I'm done with exams and I'm not sitting at home doing nothing. I need something constructive to do," Janessa grabbed a broom and started sweeping the floor. "Besides, I'd rather help you clean the toilets and the sewers and stuff than to be trying to duck and dodge Manuel all damn day."

"That boy still trying to holler at you?" Kandi asked as she moved on to the next locker to empty the papers from it, "even after you called him out at court for trying to set me up."

"Yeah, he must really think that just because I'm a big girl that I'm gonna give it up to him like I'm easy or something. He better holler at Loose Lips or something because my mama didn't raise me to do nothing like that." Janessa talked as she moved from one side of the hall to the next. "Besides, I wouldn't give it to that snitch no way."

Kandi shook her head and wondered whether or not she had created a monster. On one hand, she had come to appreciate Janessa being a witness for her and telling the judge how Cortez, Kobe and Manuel had been spreading vicious rumors about her and how they benefited from the very things she stole. That threw considerable weight when the only evidence the judge had that Kandi stole anything was the word of Manuel and his cousin and a video that didn't necessarily identify her as the thief, with her admitting that she was there, she couldn't deny it either. Since it was Kandi's first offense and because she didn't steal anything major, the judge had sentenced her to ten days in juvie so she could get a taste of what it would be like if she didn't get her act together and a thousand hours of community service to be completed before her one year probation ended. She also had to find and maintain a part time job for ninety days. As long as Kandi kept her hands clean and didn't get into no more incidents between now and graduation, the judge agreed to expunge the incident from her record since she was still sixteen.

"Hey baby," Thing had come from behind and kissed Kandi on the cheek.

"Y'all supposed to be helping, not getting me set up."

"We are, I just came by to give you your lunch so you don't have to eat the cafeteria food." Kandi was happy to see the Subway's bag with what smelled like a six inch Chicken Teriyaki sub, some potato chips, a chocolate chip cookie and a drink. "I know you get a break soon so I thought we'd spend it together."

"Aww, how sweet."

The more Kandi looked at Thing, the sexier he got. She started to appreciate the fact that Thing had brains to go with the obvious brawn. Though they've been on a few dates, they still haven't defined their relationship as boyfriend/girlfriend. Once she finished emptying the papers from the lockers, she made sure the bottles were filled with solution and started spraying the lockers so she could remove stickers, candy, hand written notes, graffiti and other nuances students seemed to keep in their lockers. Thing grabbed a bottle and started helping her on the opposite end of the hall.

When the clock struck twelve and the last exam was done for the day, they all met on Kandi's end of the hallway to enjoy their lunch. Hector, who had been cleaning the chalk boards and helping the janitors move desks in the hallways in areas of the school where exams weren't in session, joined them too.

"I see you getting a little big," Kandi noted as Hector's once frail frame began to define a little bit.

"Josiah can't be the only smart jock around here." Hector teased as he brought his arms up and flexed his muscles.

"You a mess," Kandi said, "but on the real, I appreciate y'all being here with me and doing a sister's time."

"I didn't need to stay home anyway," Thing stated, "that would have been too much temptation to try to get up with Cortez and start another brawl and I can't go back in front of that judge either. She looked out for me one time but I know she won't give me another chance."

"And I need to make sure he stays out of trouble." Hector jumped in and received more laughter.

The friends finished eating their food while talking about their plans for the summer. Hector and his parents were planning a triple to Tijuana because his father would be working on a project there for the summer. He had made arrangements with the Spanish teacher to get credit for the assignment for the upcoming school year. Janessa was going to do an office assignment with an upstart magazine so she can get more journalism experience under her belt before she started working on the school paper. Thing was hooking up with a summer program that he felt would enhance his chances of getting into UNC. Kandi was still job hunting.

"You know, Harris Teeter is hiring," Janessa said of the grocery store chain that was popular for its high quality products. "My cousin is the customer service manager, maybe I can hook you up with her."

"You think they'd take a girl who's trying to expunge a theft charge from her record?"

"You'd be surprise, they work with all kinds of people. Just get the application and I'll tell her to look for you."

Kandi smiled. Janessa had been a better friend than she could ever imagine. Maybe all girls weren't catty and gossipers after all. Once the group finished eating their food and putting their trash in the garbage, everyone went back to work. Thing has snuck to meet her in one of the classrooms where they talked a little and shared a kiss. When they were finished, they walked home to the hood, Hector and Janessa arguing over who was going to win the NBA Finals and Kandi and Thing holding hands. If everyday could be like this, maybe things wouldn't be so bad for Kandi after all.

Jarold Imes is the author of the Hold On Be Strong Teen Series. He is a graduate of North Carolina A&T State University and a resident of Winston-Salem, North Carolina.

Acknowledgements

Once again thanks to God for bringing me this far.

To my pride & joy my wife Sheena McCaulsky for holding me down and supporting me always. You're the best thing to ever happen to me Sheen. I told you we were gonna do this together and I meant that. All our dreams are going to happen. I love you Tinker Bell.

Raequel "Roxi" Edgerson, thank you for going out of your way for us. Once again I gotta thank you for letting me borrow some episodes from your life in order to create "Raina". That night of UNO and Truth or Dare we'll never forget. I know you ain't used to being thanked but you know how we are! We love ya, we're family. Like I keep on saying "Diary Confessions" is coming soon!!!

Jarold Imes, my partner in crime. Thank you for reaching out to me for this project. Your knowledge and insight has been invaluable throughout this whole process. Your work ethic and professionalism has been unmatched by anyone I've worked with in this industry. Without you and Abednegos Free I'm not sure "Real Love" would've seen the light of day. Thank you my friend. Continue to support others and they will support you.

To my mother, Zelpha I love you. Just sit back and relax and let me take care of you now. My father Lloyd, I love you dad don't forget that. My sisters Joanne & Sandra McCaulsky, I love you and I can't wait to spend some time with you all. My brother Trevor, I know we haven't had the chance to get to know each other but that doesn't stop the love and bond we got. We're Family forever. Kendra McCaulsky, I love you girl ... we didn't always get along when you were younger but I'm glad were closer now. Take care of my grand nieces! Man I feel old. RIP Michael McCaulsky.

Heath McKinney, you're more than my best friend, you're my brother. You've always had my back and you know I got yours for life ... now go put a hat on! LOL ... love you man.

Alberto "Tito" Ramos, you're my brother from another mother. Man if I can be half the father to my kids that you are to yours then I know I'm doing something right. We gonna make our dreams come true. Much love to Yaritza (Yari) (hope you don't mind LOL). My main man Draven, keep reading them comics! Love you Gaby and Nina! Mike Malcolm, what's up cuz! We gotta hook back up and get caught up with each other man. It's been too long. The same goes for you Marvin Malcolm! Tamara, Grenville and Gabrielle Beattie our friends for life. Damaris DeJesus, remember, God never closes one door without opening another! See ya soon! Jenise Anderson & Tamar Humes, it's been too long since I've seen you. And I know I haven't been back to Jamaica for a while Tamar but you ain't been to the ATL ever so don't start LOL....

England:
Rashida Malcolm, I miss you cuz. You're my little sister forever. Take care of the kids. Charelene Malcolm, I miss you too. You make me feel at home when I'm with you. Take care of Wayne and the kids. Shout out to Adam Malcolm, Daniel "Bigga" Malcolm, and Joan Sharp. I love y'all. (And all my cousins in the UK)

Beatrice Campbell (mum), I can't believe you read *The Pink Palace* mum! You're too much for me LOL... love you. Shaun Campbell, my twin (Nov 10th) I forgot ya last time but I got ya bro! I hope you enjoy this one too! Sharon Campbell, my big sister, stay happy. That's all that matters. Kaisha & Rhianna Campbell, I miss you both! See you soon! Catriona Mills, I love you girl. Thanks for letting me have your best friend. I hope you enjoy your character in the book LOL.

My back in the day friends I lost contact with I haven't forgot y'all, Patty Mitchell, Shameqe & Shamere Baugh (my twin sisters), Jenelle Smalling, Mario Miller, Alton Rogers, Ron "Double R" Gaines, Shadcore & Tonya (A, Y Not). Krystal Robinson aka Special K! Swiyyah Muhammad keep doing your thing!

Cynthia "Mocha" Parker, my friend. You're so talented that it's scary! I can't wait to read your book, with your name on it. You've taught me so much about this game and about what a great editor does. You're the shit!

Juanita Ramos aka Entrigue you are the only one for "From Vixen 2 Diva". You're so Harlem!

To my hardcore fans that showed me love from the jump off! Shanequa Pickering aka BKFinest (told ya I got ya), Yolanda Mickles aka Lady La my lil' sis, Cherron Gray-Gilmore, Trap Girl, Lady Taurus, Nesha Pooh, Andrea Denise (Thanks for the outstanding feedback!) D. Frazier "Urban Fiction Queen", Mz. Thickness- thank you! Reydee- outta Cali, Kjazzy, L.B "America Most Wanted", Butterfly02148 thanks for your support, Chocolate Girl, Ladyscorpio in Brooklyn! L. a - D. i. v. a. & C.O.R.E.Y.- keep on writing!

Thank you to all the book clubs that supported me, Reader's Paradise Book Club, The RAWSISTAZ, APOOO Book Club, Distinct Ladies Book Club, SiStar Tea at ARC Book Club Inc., Literary Vixen Book Club, The Writer's Inn, and Urban Reviews.

The authors I came into this game with Renita "Goldie" Walker & K. Roland Williams lets make history. Ben Blaze, you're the truth bruh! Thank you Tracy Brown for all your advice. Toy Styles & Deja King you two keep me motivated to write better. Priscilla V. Sales, I can never thank you enough! You were more of a mentor to me than anyone else. Eric Jerome Dickey thanks for the inspiration. Vickie Stringer thanks for my start. Marcus Williams at Nubian Bookstore thank you for looking out for me. Medu Bookstore in Atlanta, thank you for your support. And to anyone who has helped me, gave me advice and support, thank you all.

3-14-09

The SHOUT OUT

First give honor to God for allowing me to multi-task and attempt to do multiple projects at one time. I thank Jesus for setting the example of the way I am supposed to live me life. If I could only have one day in which I live my life the way you intended I know that I will have done good. And to the Holy Spirit for leading me and guiding me along the way and for finding me when I step out of bounds and taking me back again and again.

To Mom and Dad ... we are building this empire one day at a time. Jordan and Sha'Ron, I hope you guys continue to have *Love & Life* together. To Mikalia ... I am the mean uncle ... that is true. I love you. Aunt Doris and Reg for continuing to bail me out and supporting me. Grandma Peoples, I am enjoying the time we are spending together and thanks for continuing to teach me my history. Love for the Imes, Phelps, Simmons, Peoples, Brown, Carter, Braggs, Tinsley and Odom families.

Marlon ... thank you for being one of the first authors who answered my many "Calls for Submissions." I did not know this book would turn out like this and to say that I'm excited would be an understatement. They are not going to be ready for us. I can't wait for the rest of the readers to see the light on the next teen book.

Victoria Vanee Anderson, thanks for being the first author signed to my label and for giving me a chance to publish your teen work. I am looking forward to seeing both *Lady Vicious* and *Just Me & You* in print. Ben Blaze & K. Roland Williams, they are not going to be ready for y'all in *Romance for the Streets*. J. Well Speaks (formerly the crew known as CatXcan) ... I wish you guys much success as you step out as editors and thanks for letting me be part of your team. Get them projects, make that money and make us ALL look good. Marcenia, thank you for all that you have done to help me keep foot in the industry. You have been one of the easiest professionals to work with and I wish you much love and success wherever you go. Elissa Gabrielle for giving me another opportunity to be published in *Soul of a Man: The Triumph of My Soul II*. Deja King and T. Styles for answering all of my questions and continuing to elevate the bar for where it is supposed to be for authors in this game. Rumont TeKay for showing me love and for putting me on in Wisconsin. Zane, Mark Anthony and Carl Weber for taking the time to lay the foundation so that my company would have a professional blueprint to follow. Wahida Clark for my first endorsement and for continuing to have my back as I write what is in my heart. KaShamba Williams for doing the thing first.

To the editors and staff at TheUrbanBookSource.com, I owe y'all a book. I appreciate you guys for continuing to give me a platform to share m thoughts and opinions with the world. To my friends at UrbanBridgez.com (congrats on that partnership with Sister 2 Sister Magazine) and MiddleChildPromotions.com, just because I'm gone does not mean you aren't forgotten.

To the students at North Carolina Agricultural & Technical State University and Winston-Salem State University … one of y'all need to win the MEAC. '06! To the brothers of Alpha Phi Alpha Fraternity, Inc and PHI-SKEE to my lovely and soPHIsticated sorors of Alpha Kappa Alpha Sorority, Inc. Much love and respect to the other seven frats and sororities in the Pan. To the 12th House, it is the HOUSE the others stand on.

Special love to the staff and students of Goldsboro High School for letting me come into your school and share my work with you. This is one of the projects I promised you.

Last but not least, to all the readers who continue to support Marlon and myself on book after book. I hope we gave you a project you can be proud of, pray for us, and continue to support our literary endeavors.

In Unity,

Jarold Imes

FREE Order Abednego's Free Teen Titles!!!
SEND THIS ORDER TO:

NAME:_____

ADDRESS:_____

CITY/STATE:_____

ZIP:_____

EMAIL:_____

	TITLES	PRICE
	Worth Fighting 4 by Jarold Imes	$10.99
	U Can't Break Me by Jarold Imes	$10.99
	5 Miles to Empty by Jarold Imes	$10.99
	Age Ain't Nothing But a Number by Jarold Imes	$10.99
	Lessons Learned by Jarold Imes	$10.99
	Never Too Much – The Remix by Jarold Imes	$10.99
	Hold On Be Strong by Jarold Imes	$10.99
	Rollin' Wit The Punches by Jarold Imes	$10.99
	Love & Life by Marlon McCaulsky & Jarold Imes	$10.99
	Just Me & You by Victoria Vanee Anderson	$10.99
	Any book shipped to schools, teachers, students or prisons receive 25% off the retail price. Must supply a copy of the license, student id, proof of admission or register # to honor discount.	$8.24
	Shipping & Handling (1 Copy)	$2.95
	Additional Copies	$1.00
	Total	

Send Institutional Checks or Money Order to:

Abednego's Free, LLC 380-H Knollwood Street, Suite #138
Winston-Salem, North Carolina 27103
Please allow up to 2 weeks for delivery! Can also order @ HoldOnBeStrong.com

JUST ME &YOU

Victoria Vanee' Anderson

Also Available